PAWNS OF POWER

When Sir Humphrey Benford presented his widowed daughter, Marian, at Court, by order of King Edward IV, she found herself drawn into the company of Lady Anne Neville, daughter of the Earl of Warwick. Marian hoped to find a husband of her own choice, but Sir Humphrey was commanded by the King to wed her to Sir Ralf Compton. The Lady Anne was in love with the King's younger brother, Richard of Gloucester, but her father had quarrelled with the King. How could either girl seek to win free from the chess game of power played by her father?

Books by Joanna Makepeace
in the Linford Romance Library:

MY LORD ENEMY

JOANNA MAKEPEACE

◆

PAWNS
OF
POWER

Complete and Unabridged

LINFORD
Leicester

First published in Great Britain in 1972

First Linford Edition
published 2003

British Library CIP Data

Makepeace, Joanna, 1927 –
    Pawns of power.—Large print ed.—
Linford romance library
1. Love stories
2. Large type books
I. Title
823.9'14 [F]

ISBN 0–7089–9476–8

Published by
F. A. Thorpe (Publishing)
Anstey, Leicestershire

Set by Words & Graphics Ltd.
Anstey, Leicestershire
Printed and bound in Great Britain by
T. J. International Ltd., Padstow, Cornwall

This book is printed on acid-free paper

Part I

1

Marian gazed fixedly ahead determined to ignore Janet's frigid immobility as she sat opposite, seemingly impervious to the jolts and sways of the carriage over the hardened ruts of the road. If the woman was angered by her sudden decision to return to the city, she must learn to accept her mistress's whims. Marian had had quite enough of the outspoken disapproval of others to last her a lifetime.

She had mourned Matthew Hurst well over the customary year. It was almost sixteen months since he had died and she had buried herself in his country house in Kent with his grieving sister for company. During all that time there had been no word from her father. Well, she would wait no longer. The last exchange of biting words this morning had finished the matter. She would go back to the shop. Her conduct could not now be deemed unbecoming in a merchant's widow. Janet would be forbidding enough to frighten off any young sprig who would wish to accost her. The house was large and full of servants, apprentices and poor relations. She would be amply chaperoned even if Sir Humphrey did not fulfil his promise and ride down from Northamptonshire to keep her company. The corners of her lips twitched and Janet's frown grew even blacker. If Marian were any judge it would be difficult to *prevent* her father from thrusting himself upon her in the fine town house she had inherited as part of the fortune Matthew had left her.

Poor Matthew — it would have been easier if she could have borne his nearness. His touch had repelled her, though he had striven to please. Nearing sixty and a widower he had fallen deeply in love with her that time her father had taken her to buy silk for her first court gown. Sir Humphrey Benford had hated to admit, even then, that a temporary shortage of funds made it impossible to allow her choice of Matthew Hurst's finest brocades and velvets. The man's eyes had lighted on Marian's proud upright carriage and just the hint of red-gold hair which showed under the frontal of her hennin. He had been obsequious in his anxiety to extend credit.

Sir Humphrey must not excuse himself. He must allow Mistress Marian to have what she desired. Payment could be made later — much later. Hurst had spread his hands wide in a gesture deprecating Sir Humphrey's concern. Mistress Marian's beauty should not be overlooked at the court of King Edward. His Queen, the former Lady Grey's, fair beauty was a by-word. Even her golden loveliness would be dimmed by Mistress Marian's youth and freshness. Now the rich green velvet, the brown and gold shot silk from Damascus would enrich her vital colouring . . .

And so it had begun. At first Sir Humphrey's thin lips had curled with contempt for the ageing, corpulent little merchant. But the man had been generous and accommodating. Marian was still so very young and his only child. The Wars had impoverished him. His own extravagant nature had finally beggared them. Their lodgings in Honey Lane were bare and to Marian's fastidious soul hardly as clean as she had wished. Yet her father preferred to remain in London as a hanger-on at court. Marian was not, however, to wear her finery at Westminster. Since his sympathies had been known to be with the Lancastrian cause, her father was in no great favour with Edward of York. The Queen had known him some years previously, had some affection for his wife and had expressed herself pleased to welcome Marian to court, though she could offer no place among her ladies as he had hoped, but the King remained obdurate and refused to receive them. Increasing poverty loomed up at him and Matthew Hurst's infatuation for his daughter was a blessing he could ill afford to ignore.

Marian was used to obedience. Her father had more than once enforced it with his whip. She had spoken, dry mouthed, of her objection to the match. It had gained her nothing and at last she had married Matthew Hurst at the Church of St. Mary Magdalen and thrust firmly aside her revulsion at his grossness and the moist soft feel of his hands on her body. Indeed, pity made her anxious to hide her distress, for Matthew had worshipped her to the disapproval of his vinegary sister. He had offered her all that money could buy and she had tried her hardest to be the wife he expected.

The house behind the shop in the Chepe was more richly furnished than their own home in Northamptonshire. Her gowns were finer than her father could have purchased. Matthew Hurst continued to treat his child-bride with loving patience and she had been content to live quietly with him in London and, during the hot months when the plague was rife in the city, at his pleasant country house in Kent.

Death had taken him suddenly. One day he was bustling about in his kindly officious manner in the shop, and the next he lay paralysed in his bed, unable to speak or move.

She had tended him well, but the physician had shaken his head, despairing of recovery, and a week later he'd died.

Sir Humphrey Benford had not troubled to hide his relief. His daughter was now a rich widow, lovely, unencumbered by children. He could hope for a more advantageous marriage. On this subject he was cautious. Marian must not grieve. She had done all that she should and more. She must go into the country for her period of mourning. He would see that business progressed well at the shop. In the hands of Nicholas Blake, her husband's assistant, affairs would pursue their normal course.

Later he would summon her back to the city and she could resume her old life — perhaps be presented at court. In his heart he doubted that last statement. Edward borrowed from his merchant acquaintances, slept with their wives, but they were *never* received at court. Setting aside this trifling obstacle, he had hopes of a suitable match for Marian. Not that he would mention this to the lass. She had obeyed him once. Now she dreamed, as all wenches did, of a freedom of choice. When the time came she'd prove docile enough.

A sudden bone-shaking jolt almost threw them onto the floor of the carriage. Angrily Janet swept aside the leathern curtain and shouted to Walter Boles, their coachman. Once before their journey had been interrupted by an iron pin coming loose and they'd been forced to sit in a mean hostelry for two hours while Walter and a half-witted lad from the village had worked on the wheel. Their baggage wagons had passed them on the road hours since. At the time Walter had expressed doubts that the repair would last satisfactorily. It seemed now that his gloomy forebodings had proved correct.

He came to the window, peered in anxiously, his hand scratching at his greying thatch of hair.

'The wheel's off, mistress. I feared it would happen. Fortunately we are in the city now. If you'll wait here, I'll try to order a litter for you.'

Marian allowed the exasperation she felt to colour her answer. 'Oh Walter, not again. You really should have made a fair job of it before. You took long enough.' She could have wished to bite back her words when she saw his distress. The old man was fond of her and his silent sympathy had been one of her consolations during the difficult time she'd spent with her sister-in-law.

'Sorry, mistress. I tried, but I said at the time we'd be lucky if it held. It's late but we're not far from home. I'll get you a carriage. You shouldn't have to wait long.'

'I should think not.' Janet's tart tones came from behind her. 'The conveyance should have been checked over for faults before we began this journey.'

Marian grimaced. She knew Janet would have added a rider that the journey should have not been undertaken at all had she dared.

'That will be enough said on the matter, Janet,' she said coldly. 'Walter has done his best, I'm sure.' She held out her arms to the coachman. 'Help me down, Walter, I'm stiff with sitting.'

'Aye, mistress.'

She sighed her relief that they were nearer home than she had thought. 'Why it will take us less than half an hour to walk. The night is not cold. Come, Janet, we'll go on foot.'

Janet was scandalised and said as much. 'At this hour, mistress? You'd be foolish to attempt it.'

'I am getting very tired of hearing how foolish and immature I am, Janet.'

Marian's voice was now ice-cold. 'Nevertheless, I am Matthew Hurst's widow and mistress over my own house and servants. In the future if they prefer to disobey my instructions or are uneasy as to my ability to superintend my own household, they will be at liberty to seek employment elsewhere.'

Janet Thurston's severe expression almost crumpled into one of extreme distress. 'Mistress Hurst, I meant no disrespect. If . . . '

'Then please, Janet, come down and let us get on.'

Walter was torn between desire to remain with his beloved horses and to ensure the safety of the carriage and his concern for his mistress's safety.

'I could escort you and then come back but . . . '

'No, Walter, no need. In the city we are under the protection of the Watch. Stay with the carriage.'

'There are footpads, lady, and some-times . . . '

'I know, I know, but I'm young and

fleet of foot and Janet is strong enough for anything or so she is constantly assuring me. We can be home very quickly. If the baggage is safely disposed, which I am sure it is by now, they will send out apprentices with torches to await us.'

'Aye, mistress.'

She touched his hand and he looked anxiously into her grey eyes, sparkling now with an added zest. For so long those eyes had lacked lustre and the corners of her wide mouth had turned downwards in despondency. At last she was back in London and she had no intention of remaining docilely in the carriage until relief arrived. She was tired of being treated as a spineless doll with no will of her own.

'I shall be safe enough, Walter. The torches are still alight in the streets and there are few people about at this hour.'

He nodded though without enthusiasm.

Marian turned to Janet who was wrapping her cloak round her for comfort and staring uneasily at the shuttered houses and shops.

'Are you ready?'

The older woman nodded, her expression mutinous.

'Then let us begin.'

Marian set the pace, Janet padding stolidly behind. She was glad they were near to London Bridge since the soles of her fine leather boots were thin and not made for walking on the cobbles of the town. Janet muttered something under her breath as she slipped on some refuse carelessly cast into the street. Marian refrained from turning to assist her as she knew if she did so, she would be treated to a display of righteous indignation or a torrent of words again decrying the foolhardiness of walking the short distance unescorted. She went on determinedly and at last Janet caught her up, once more silent.

The streets in this quarter were quiet enough, the houses shuttered, torches at the corners giving a spluttering unsteady light. There was some moonlight though the night was cloudy, and Marian knew her way. As they drew closer to the river the signs of life were more apparent to the ear. Open tavern doors disgorged roisterers, drunken but for the most part in good humour. Stinks of ale and vomit smote the air and bawdy comments were levelled at the two women. Marian held her head high and ignored the revellers. Janet sniffed loudly enough to be heard by her mistress who was well in front. Marian plunged down an alley, anxious to be well away from the taverns and brothels. Soon she would be home. Despite her brave words to Janet, her heart-beats had become louder and more rapid as she crossed the darkened streets. She had been cloistered in the country of late. She had forgotten the sights and sounds of London after dark. In truth she had never been out so late before not accompanied by her father or several household servants. Janet panted along behind, winded by Marian's increased pace. At first Marian thought the two shadows which lurked along the houses were figments of her imagination, conjured up by her own fears. They made no sound and when she cast one hurried glance they had disappeared into the shadow of an overhead gable. Janet seemed intent now on watching her way lest she slip again or wrench her ankle on a boulder or loosened cobblestone. She passed no comment and Marian hurried on. She had been mistaken — she *must* have been mistaken.

One choking gasp behind her gave her pause. She turned on the instant to find Janet struggling in the grip of one of their shadowy followers. Too late she glimpsed the other before he reached out to grasp her. She gave a shrill scream before his hand clamped hard over her mouth. Desperately she fought, her hands clawing up at his hand and down his face causing him to mutter an oath. He was thin but wiry. She was aware of his stinking breath hot on her face. She kicked out blindly and knew the satisfaction of hearing her attacker smother a cry. Momentarily he released his hold and she seized her opportunity and ran hard across the street. She knew he would follow and he was stronger and faster. Though heavier he was used to moving quickly and her skirts and fine soft boots hampered her. Crying hysterically she reached the first house and hammered on the door, hardly knowing herself what she screamed.

The door opened abruptly and she half fell into the arms of a man who opened it. He was a big man. His huge frame filled the doorway and she staggered against him in her fear, reassured by his bulk and the ease of movement as he steadied her against his shoulder.

'Easy, easy, lass. No cause for alarm. This door isn't barred against wenches, I assure you.'

She didn't look up at him. Dimly she was aware that the hall was lighted and that other men had come up behind him.

'Please, I beg of you. Footpads

attacked us in the street. My servant
— she's elderly . . . '

Easily he placed her on a stool inside.
'Steady there. Leave this to us. It's all
over — nothing to fear. Frank, Will,' he
called to two of his companions. 'Come
with me.'

She sat huddled on the stool sobbing
with fear and relief while the men
rushed by her. If her life depended on
the outcome she could not have gone to
Janet's assistance now. Even in her
half-crazed state she blamed herself for
Janet's plight. The attack had come so
quickly and she'd panicked without
thought of the other woman whom
she'd led into danger, yet what could
she have done?

Something cool was placed against
her hand. She started like a frightened
hare and stared upwards at the man
who'd come to her side and was
offering her a pewter tankard.

'Drink this. You'll feel better.'

'Janet . . . '

'My comrades will rescue her. If I

thought they needed my aid I would have accompanied them.'

She gulped down the malmsey and put a hand to her shaking lips. 'I'm sorry. I acted like a fool. I'm not usually so stupid. Thank you.'

He shrugged. He was a tall man, slim and elegantly dressed, his dark hair curling onto the collar of his doublet.

'One's wits are like to desert one at such a time. I hardly considered you craven. You came for assistance. It was the simplest and most effective way to help your maid.'

She gave a watery smile and he took the tankard from her and moved away. His walk was unhurried, assured, turning as the big man who'd opened the door came back into the house.

'All is safe, mistress. Your maid is frightened but unhurt. One of the rogues escaped. Frank caught the other. He will deal with him and hand him into charge. Will comes more slowly with your woman.'

His bold blue eyes raked over her and

she flushed hotly under his appraisal, aware all at once of her gown and shift torn across the bosom and revealing one firm swelling young breast. She lowered her eyes and, tugged the material close in a useless attempt to order the disarray.

'Thank you, sir. I cannot thank you enough. I . . . I was foolish to walk unescorted. My carriage . . . '

'No apologies needed. You gave us unexpected sport. Eh, Ralf?' The big man turned to the dark man who'd offered his comfort.

'Aye, sir.' The slim tall man let his eyes rest for a second on Marian's frightened face and he regarded the other steadily.

A whispering and half-smothered giggle came from a stairway behind her and Marian looked up to see two scantily robed ladies peeping down at her. The big man looked up following her gaze, the corners of his lazy mouth twitching at sight of them. 'So, we have reinforcements. The lady might welcome your assistance.'

The dark man whom he'd addressed as Ralf, said coolly, 'I think it wiser if Mistress . . . ' he paused as Marian was about to give her name, then made a small gesture of his hand cautioning her to silence, 'were to return home at once, sir. She is in mourning I see. Her relatives will be disturbed at her continued absence.'

The huge fair man checked at his words and looked at her again, his eyes less lazy, more shrewd now, taking in her mourning gown of costly silk and the black veil on her hennin.

'Indeed I am grieved you should have suffered this extra trouble, Mistress . . . '

He waited deliberately for her to supply her name. She looked helplessly towards her adviser who shrugged again.

'I am Mistress Hurst, Marian Hurst. My husband died over a year ago. I have been in Kent at the country house and was returning with Janet to the

21

shop in Chepeside. You have my undying gratitude, sir.'

The big man laughed back at Ralf. 'You see, my lad, you get nothing by remaining here in the shelter of the shop while we go to the rescue. Here's Will back with Janet is it?'

Ralf smiled faintly. He seemed unperturbed by the other's jibe.

'I believed, and rightly so, that you did not require my assistance, sir, and I will win my gratitude by offering my escort to the lady to her home.'

'Well said, Ralf.' The man's frame shook with his mirth. It was clear that these two were accustomed to this verbal sparring and always remained the best of friends regardless.

'Sir Ralf Compton will see you both safely home, mistress, unless your maid would prefer to rest awhile.'

Janet, supported by the arm of another elegantly dressed gentleman, looked sharply round the room and upwards at the two women on the stair. She stood upright at once and coldly declined the need to rest. 'No, no. I'm recovered. We must go. I thank you, sir.'

The fair giant smiled. Marian thought he was god-like in his splendour, though he was less gorgeously clad than his friends. His grin was infectious and though she knew she should be circumspect, she found herself responding with an answering smile.

'You have been kind, sir. My father will wish to reward you if . . . '

He countered her question smoothly as he raised her hand to his lips. 'When we meet I will remind him of his debt, lady. Never fear. Now go with Sir Ralf or I shall not wish to part with your company.'

Recognising his innate nobility, she curtseyed and passed out of the house with Sir Ralf. On the threshold he enveloped her in his cloak and she cast him one glance of profound gratitude.

2

Sir Ralf Compton frowned as his squire opened the door of his apartment, then stood gossiping on the threshold with some page or servant outside in the corridor. The noise, as a group of courtiers clattered by, the men's voices loud and seemingly aggressive and the high-pitched laughter of the women, resounded in his aching head as if an army of carpenters were busy erecting a scaffold just above his eyes. He called to the lad sharply.

'Simon, close the door.'

The boy came sullenly to his side and Compton averted his eyes. Simon Wentworth had been with him some two months now and his dislike of his master seemed as strong as ever. He was a big youth, broad and shambling, his hair thick and ashen fair, his complexion florid, and just now bearing one or two pimples and blotches of adolescence. His father had been a former comrade. They had served together as mercenaries for a time at the Burgundian court. For his sake he'd agreed to take the lad and introduce him at court. Simon was a good squire, he learned his skill at arms well, was efficient with sword and lance and had a good seat on horseback, but he'd no charm. He resented the hours waiting on Compton, learning the courtly grace required of a gentleman. He'd been bred in the harsher air of the North and he missed the farms and rough sea breezes of his native Yorkshire. He looked now with distaste at Compton's doublet and hose of elegant cut on the stool near his bed. His young mouth almost betrayed a sneer. Surely his father might have chosen a true knight for him, one whose courage in the field could never be doubted, not this scented bejewelled fop who appeared to prefer to spend his time in the King's company wenching and drinking rather than in the more sober pursuits of jousting and hunting.

'What hour is it?' Compton's question was brusque.

'Well past noon, sir. The King has been asking for you.'

'So?' Compton's eyebrows rose. His brown eyes met the lad's directly. 'When did you receive the message?'

'Not an hour ago, sir.'

'It has taken you long enough to wake me.'

'The page said the matter was not urgent. You came to bed so late, sir . . . ' The boy's tone indicated that a more apt word would have been 'early'. He paused before adding coolly, 'I thought it better to let you sleep.'

Compton rose and reached for a bed robe, thrusting his arms into the wide furred sleeves. 'Allow me to be the judge of the urgency of any summons from His Grace the King. Is my bath ready?'

'Aye, sir.'

'The King rides this afternoon? Do you know?'

'No, sir. The page indicated that he

would relax in his private chamber. He will receive you then.'

Compton grunted and sauntered into the next room where a serving man waited with a large jug of cold water, and steam hissed from a bath prepared for him on the stone floor. He stepped in and scrubbed away at the stink of sweat and stale scent of the previous night's carousing.

The King grinned at him amiably as he presented himself later. Compton almost winced at sight of him. No amount of carousing appeared to affect him in the least. He was lolling back on a day-bed, one hand idly caressing the soft ears of the greyhound bitch at his side.

'Well, Sir Ralf, you conveyed the lady safely home, I take it?'

'Yes, Your Grace. Her servants were anxiously awaiting her arrival. The baggage wagons had appeared some hours previously. Her principal craftsman, Mr. Nicholas Blake, was beginning to fear some mishap had occurred.'

'Good, good.' The King continued to smile. Compton stood at his ease, but watched him carefully. He had not yet been invited to seat himself. Was Edward angered by last night's adventure? Under that lazy charm, the man was shrewd enough. 'Indeed the lady was so discreetly withdrawn from my company, that I doubt any spot or stain could mar her reputation despite the lateness of her return.'

Compton's eyes met the blue ones of his sovereign coolly. 'I had not thought the girl worthy enough for Your Grace's notice,' he countered smoothly. 'I am grieved if I erred in taste in cutting short your — entertainment.' The minute pause before the final word brought forth a chuckle.

'You rogue, Ralf. I'll warrant you had eyes for the lass yourself. She's comely enough.'

'True, sire, but a merchant's wife.'

'Widow, I thought she said.'

'You correct me, sire. Indeed she is a widow.'

'And very wealthy.'

'Indeed?' Compton walked gracefully over to the window seat as the King's bejewelled hand waved him to sit.

'To the tune of some ten thousand crowns. I've spent some time this morning making enquiries.'

Compton was silent and gave his attention to the jewelled chain round his neck. He had not thought the King so taken with the girl's undoubted beauty. Obviously he had miscalculated. Edward could be dangerous when crossed, particularly in his dealing with a woman.

'It is time you took a wife, Sir Ralf. It will curb these bad habits of yours.' The King's tone was mocking and Compton gave him a half bow of respect.

'Your Grace knows I am ready to please you in all things but . . . '

'Not in the choosing of a wife?' The question was more sharply edged and Compton raised his eyes once more to the blue ones opposite, stung by the determination of the King's tone.

'Even in that, sire — if . . . '

'Then you would not be averse to pleasing me in this matter?'

'I have said as much, sire.'

'This girl, Mistress Marian Hurst, is the daughter of Sir Humphrey Benford. You know the man?'

Compton inclined his head. 'I have met him once or twice only.'

'His allegiance is to Lancaster. He took the field at Mortimer's Cross.'

'He was in favour at King Henry's court?'

'At first he was well received but the man is extravagant, a gambler. Our saintly Harry disapproved of his ways and dismissed him from court. The Queen, however, encouraged him.'

'He married his daughter to a cloth merchant?'

'Bend that stiff spine of yours, Sir Ralf. Aye. Sir Humphrey needed Matthew Hurst's gold as much as you do on those impoverished estates of yours, and as much as I am anxious to see that gold is not misused against me.

Do you catch my drift? I'm sure you do, Ralf.'

Compton did indeed, only too clearly. The King leaned forward to peer at him intently. 'Shall I put the matter plainly? It would please me if you were to wed the girl. Well?'

'My faults are many. I have never sought to hide them but I am not one who would force a maid to an unwilling match.'

The King's eyes passed quickly over the elegant figure seated stiffly now in the window seat, the dark eyes stormy under frowning brows. 'Come, Sir Ralf, if you are so minded, I doubt if you could not bring the widow to a suitable frame of mind. You are not unattractive to women. You have studied the art and I have not found you wanting in skill.'

'Sir Humphrey?'

'He can be brought to see reason. He would have no objections if his daughter were to become a countess.'

Compton's chin jerked up abruptly and the King sat back again and resumed his stroking of the greyhound, which relaxed and surrendered itself to sensual pleasure under his hand.

'Aye, you heard me correctly. I will give you an earldom if you give way to my wishes in this matter.'

Compton rose and crossed to the King's side. 'This is so important to you then?'

Edward nodded briefly. 'I would have the gold in safe hands. I discussed the girl this morning with Will Hastings. He informed me that she's Benford's wench and of the size of her fortune. Hurst died sixteen months ago or near enough that time. His widow will soon be out of mourning. No doubt her father will look high for her. Did she not take your eye? *I* was sufficiently interested to ask about her.'

'She is lovely.' Compton was evasive and then as the King waited for a further remark, he said, 'I prefer my women either virginal or nobly born. I had not thought to look for further acquaintance.'

'But you will do so?'

Compton's smile deepened. He gave his faintly insolent courtly bow of acquiescence. 'Aye, sir, since you wish it and you offer so fair a reward.'

'I'll give you the earldom of Saxby as your wedding gift. Get you about your wooing, man. Mistress Hurst would not be alarmed if today you visit the shop, concerned about her welfare after her misadventure of last evening. What more natural than that you should do so?'

Compton laughed without further reserve. 'Your Grace commands. I must needs obey. As you say, the lass is not without merit.'

'Well said, Sir Ralf. Make your sacrifice with good grace. There are others of my gentlemen I could try but I prefer the lass to have the best match.'

'Your Grace honours me indeed.'

'I know you well, Sir Ralf. You are rascally enough for my purpose, companion of my debauchery. Now, get you gone about your courting. In the meantime I will summon Sir Humphrey Benford to court. My Queen has spoken for the man. It is time I graciously overlooked his partisanship of the wrong cause. It will please me to receive him.'

Compton bowed again. He was smiling broadly as he withdrew.

In the corridor he stepped respectfully aside as Gloucester, the King's younger brother, made to enter the apartment. The prince's grey-green eyes regarded him coldly. Compton bowed, his own eyes lowered deferentially. The stripling held him in no favour as he had contempt for the wilder of Edward's drinking companions. Unlike George of Clarence, young Gloucester inclined to more sober pursuits. His adoration for Edward, ten years his senior, caused him to see no fault in the dissolute young monarch. Richard laid his brother's misdemeanours down to the advice of unwise counsellors. His youthful worship of the god-like Edward blinded him to the King's more obvious failings. Only recently he had come to court from Middleham where he had served Richard Neville, Earl of Warwick, as squire and learned his skill at arms. If the boy seemed pale and delicate, Ralf knew him to be strong enough and one he'd gladly serve in battle. He sighed. It was a pity the prince disliked him so markedly.

He returned to his own quarters in thoughtful mood. He was twenty-four. The King was in the right of it. He must marry and soon. His mother had reminded him many times of the need for an heir. Since his father's death she preferred to remain in the quiet seclusion of his Norfolk manor. She would welcome a daughter-in-law — but one such as Mistress Marian Hurst? He doubted her approval of the match. She looked for nobler blood from which to breed her grandchildren. But an earldom? He shrugged. What mattered it what bride he chose? If the King favoured this lass then ill become it for Ralf Compton to deny him. He called for his squire to accompany him and a grim smile hovered about his lips. Simon would not enjoy the coming months. The boy's disinclination for feminine pursuits had been made plain enough. But then Simon could no more be allowed to please himself than his betters.

3

Marian rejoiced for once in the knowledge that she was at last mistress of her own household. She set about the task of overseeing the sweeping out of the house, the laying of fresh rushes and the polishing and burnishing of dishes and pewter neglected for the long months she had been absent. Janet, almost prostrate after her terrible misadventure of last night, had kept to her room. Marian could not prevent a little glow of satisfaction sweeping over her when she withdrew from the older woman's chamber after briskly advising her to stay in her bed and rest for at least one day. It was freedom indeed to move through the house without either Matthew's sister, Susanah, or Janet at her elbow, murmuring advice or evincing signs of dissatisfaction at her every decision.

Nan Drew, the maid of all work, tripped after her, nodding sagely at her instructions and only once or twice venturing an opinion of her own. The girl had come to the shop from the parish poor house. She was a thin-faced, lathe-like figure of a child of about thirteen years of age. Even Nan had no idea of her true age, had not kept count of the lean years of suffering in the poor house. She was willing but without experience. As far as Marian could judge, the child had done well considering she had been left to her own devices for all this time. There must be other maids beside the cook who wielded a rod of iron in the kitchen and the boy who'd joined the household but recently to scrub the pots and tend the spit. Nan must have assistance. In fact, Marian had half made up her mind to employ the girl as personal maid and free her from many of the more disagreeable tasks about the house.

The garden had been neglected. She

tutted her distress at the realisation that she must purchase the herbs for the still room this year. It was a warm day and she sank down on a bench for a moment in the sunlight, allowing herself the luxury of the first rest of the day. Nan excused herself and dashed off to attend to some trifling task. The girl appeared to be in a continual flutter. She would exhaust herself. She was ill-clad and, Marian surmised, ill-fed. She must investigate the situation in the kitchen. There would be no more cheese-paring in this house, she was determined. There had been enough of that throughout her short life, first at her home in Northamptonshire then in their lodging here in London and under Susanah's charge in Kent. Matthew had spoilt her shamefully during the year of their marriage. She had not realised that the servants and apprentices were less than adequately provided for.

It was pleasant here. Her skirts were tucked up above her ankles to assist her quicker progress through the house, her tight undersleeves pushed up her arms as far as they would go, and the long oversleeves tied in loose knots out of her way. Her adventure of the previous night had fascinated rather than distressed her. True it might have ended disastrously had not help been so readily at hand. Sir Ralf Compton had been quietly attentive during the final steps to her own house and Nicholas Blake had had warming pans already passed over the sheets to welcome her. Altogether she had come out of the affair well. She chuckled as she thought of Janet's outraged reaction.

'Mistress, did you not know that house was a noted brothel? Oh, the clientele was always of the best but the service was no different from any other house.'

Marian had reminded her tartly that there had been no opportunity for choice in her appeals for assistance. The young men who'd so timely come to her aid had offered her no discourtesy.

The big fair man's eyes had appraised her boldly. She blushed even now as she thought how she must have appeared to him, unescorted and in so dishevelled a state. He could not be blamed if his opinion of her had been less than respectful. Sir Ralf Compton had ushered her out of that house quickly. She laughed suddenly. It was so absurd how men liked to believe women were not aware of their nocturnal activities. Life with her own father had left her in no doubts as to his sexual appetites.

Nan was agitated as she came back into the garden.

'A visitor — to see you, mistress.'

Marian was surprised. None knew yet she had returned to London. She rose and tugged at her skirts. She must order her appearance or at least do what was possible quickly.

'Who is it, Nan? Has word come from my father?'

'No, lady. I have never seen the man before. I thought him a customer. Sir Ralf Compton — he says . . . '

41

Marian stopped dead, her cheeks suddenly scarlet.

'Sir Ralf Compton here? You are sure, girl?'

'He gave his name, mistress — a dark man, very richly dressed . . . '

'Yes, I know. I've met the gentleman. Thank you, Nan. Is he in the solar?'

Nan nodded, her eyes round with curiosity.

'Very well. I'll see him. Bring wine — the best.'

Nan scuttled off and Marian paused for a moment as she entered the stone-flagged hall at the rear of the house. By all the saints why couldn't the man have come later or given warning? She must look like a scullery maid and there was no time to change her gown. She grimaced as she thought this would be the second time in two days he would see her looking less than her best. She smoothed her front hair back under her hennin, loosened her sleeves, still uncomfortably aware that the velvet was woefully crushed, and pushed open the door to the solar.

He rose from his bow, his brown eyes gleaming, gold touched from the sun's light reflected in the oriel window behind him. Her cheeks reddened again despite her effort to appear the calm dignified hostess. This was rank foolishness. This man should not arouse in her this state of acute awareness. He had called in customary politeness to enquire about her health, concerned after her fears of the previous night. That was all. He was as elegant as ever, his brown tunic patterned in gold, cut fashionably short, his hose tight-fitting, immaculate in grey to match his round felt hat, of the same colour. She looked swiftly at its simplicity, unadorned by jewelled clasp or plume, his black hair curling from beneath its brim. He made her feel gauche, a country maid or what she was in truth, some merchant's wife aping nobility. Today in fact she could not even claim that excuse. In this worn gown he would take her for some upper servant, rather than mistress in her own right.

'You are welcome. Sir Ralf.' To her own ears her voice sounded breathless, unlike itself. 'Please sit down. I am pleased so soon to be able to see you and fittingly express my gratitude.'

His smile was slow, his manner, despite his dress, devoid of affectation.

'I was anxious to assure myself that all is well. You seem in good spirits, mistress. How is your woman?'

'Oh — she is tired and distressed, I think. I blame myself, sir. I should not have attempted the walk at that hour unescorted.'

His lips twitched. 'You have said that already. Put it from your mind, lady. It ill becomes you to continue to make excuses. Your own courage was reason enough.'

She smiled her relief at his understanding. 'Call it foolhardiness, sir.'

'If you wish.'

Again she laughed, her embarrassment forgotten in his own teasing manner. It was a long time since she had been allowed to be herself or to express her amusement. With this man she felt at home and it aurgured well for her intention to remain in her own house, subject only to her own desires.

His next question touched on what she had been thinking. 'You are pleased to be back in London?'

She nodded. 'The house in Kent is very charmingly situated but we have been in mourning. The time has come now for me to seek a new way of life for myself.'

'There were no children of your marriage?'

Colour crept up her throat and cheeks. 'No, my husband was elderly. We were scarce married a year.'

'Unpleasant for you.' His comment was dryly uttered and she felt the need to come to her husband's defence.

'Matthew was a good man and sought only my happiness. A sudden stroke paralysed him. I could not in mercy wish him to go on living as he was.'

'But the business prospers, I see.'

'Yes, Master Nicholas Blake, whom you met last night, you will remember, is an excellent business man. Affairs can be safely left in his hands. I have asked the lawyers to draft a deed of partnership.'

'Will you continue to live here without some male relative to advise you?'

Again she flushed. 'My father is to come up from Northamptonshire. He has promised to stay with me.'

He rose smiling. 'Then I can but hope that in time you will emerge from your mourning and live more pleasantly, mistress. London is a gay place now that the quarrels at court are over. The King gives a lead to his subjects in merriment.'

Her eyes sparkled. 'So I have heard.'

'You have never seen the King?'

'I was not presented at court. I was to have been . . . ' she broke off uncertainly, 'but some problem arose. My father could not take me then and later I married.'

He was regarding her thoughtfully and she frowned. She had the odd feeling that he was laughing at her for some reason, though his expression continued to be grave enough.

'I will take my leave. You must be tired after yesterday's ride and the unfortunate ending of your journey. I hope I have your leave to call again.'

She curtseyed. 'Certainly, sir. I am sure my father will be pleased to extend the invitation when I explain to him how you assisted me.'

'My companion was of more help, mistress.'

'Of practical help, perhaps, but . . . ' she paused and smiled shyly, 'it was you who gave understanding when I most needed it.'

She accompanied him into the shop where Simon Wentworth awaited him. She found the boy's pale blue eyes disconcerting as his gaze swept over her. He gave her the impression he had searched her and found her wanting.

As Compton moved to the door, it was jerked open and Sir Humphrey Benford hurried into the shop. It was obvious to Marian in that moment that he was in a fury. His mouth was set in the familiar tight line but his eyes were steely. He stopped abruptly at sight of her guest.

'Father, I am pleased you have come,' she said quickly. 'Sir Ralf Compton is just leaving. He was able to do me a service yesterday, for which I shall be ever grateful. He called in courtesy to ask after my health.'

Benford bowed coldly. 'You have my thanks, sir. As no doubt you see, my daughter is mourning her husband.'

'And it is close to the end of that period, I understand, sir. I shall look forward to seeing her in the city.'

Compton bowed again and withdrew. Benford turned angrily to face her.

'What is that popinjay doing here? Had he come to buy cloth I might have understood it, but I see him paying you compliments.'

'Should that be so strange?' She was surprised to note the grating quality of her own tone. 'I am young enough still, despite the fact I am a widow.'

'Aye, a *merchant's* widow. That young fop has aspirations too high for your class.'

'It is the class into which you sold me.'

His eyes glinted oddly in the shade of the shop. 'Have you grown sharp teeth in Kent, my girl? You're my child still and owe me obedience.'

'I owe you respect *if* you earn it.' She drew back as he came towards her. 'Let us not quarrel, father. We need each other. You will still want money I've no doubt and I have need of you as my protector.'

'You dare to speak to me thus and to leave Kent without my leave . . . '

'I am mistress in my own house, don't forget,' she interrupted him sharply. 'You no longer have undisputed rights over me. I married once at your bidding. I'll do so again when *I* am ready and according to the dictates of my own heart. Matthew left his gold to me. Never fear that I will grant you some share of it but do not seek to compel me.'

'Should a child speak so to her father?'

'I do not know.' She made a weary gesture of her hand. 'Perhaps not, but come in. As I said I am glad you are here but I have listened to enough sermons for my own good. I'll hear no more.'

'This man, Compton . . . '

'I'll tell you of him later. I was attacked in the street. He helped me.'

He looked past her at the door. 'You liked what you saw of him?'

She shrugged lightly. 'I have seen so few young men in the last months. I would find any of them god-like in his splendour. He seemed pleasing enough.'

'He's in Edward's favour.'

'Received well at court?'

'Aye. He's not the fool he looks and the King needs friends these days to support him against Warwick. Perhaps it is well he came here. Who knows, we may need him.'

'For what?'

Benford smiled, the thin lips baring over his teeth in a rare sign of benevolence. 'Naught that concerns you, lass. Come in and call your servants to bring food. Since I received your last letter I've made haste to come to you.'

She was frowning as she preceded him to the parlour, but she knew him well enough not to press him too soon to reveal what was in his mind.

4

It was hot in Westminster Great Hall and Marian stood uncertainly among the Queen's ladies, her eyes searching the ranks of those around the King for a sight of her father. Her cheeks burned with the agony of embarrassment through which she had just passed. How could His Grace the King have treated her thus — or Sir Ralf Compton in whom she had trusted? Why had he not warned her of what was to come?

Her father had been as surprised as she when the King's letter had arrived bidding him to court at last and to bring with him his daughter, Mistress Marian Hurst. Benford had frowned over the missive, turning it first one way and then another in his fingers, as he struggled to read what lay behind the King's gracious invitation. He had long waited for this and it had been denied him. Edward remembered too well his allegiance to Queen Margaret, though King Harry's saintly ways had irritated him to the point of desperation. Now His Grace chose to summon him to court. Doubtless he was anxious to cultivate all men who would prove a bulwark against Warwick becoming yet more threatening in his attitude towards his young monarch. Edward's marriage to the former Lancastrian, Lady Elizabeth Grey, had angered him. Had not he, Neville of Warwick, been made to look a crass fool in the courts of Europe in his anxiety to betroth his King to Bona of Savoy only to be recalled to Westminster and informed that Edward had chosen his own bride, and to rub salt in the wound, that bride the widow of a former enemy? Furious exchanges had been made, behind locked doors though they be. It was clear to Warwick he could no longer control the pleasure-loving Edward. Sullenly he waited at his northern castle of Middleham for the King to give a sign that he would once more return to the attitude of gratitude he, Warwick, considered his right. Had he not *made* Edward King after Mortimer's Cross? By the Holy Rood, if that did not suffice to make the man duly benevolent to his loyal subject, he'd make other kings. The atmosphere at court was tense and the King, outwardly undeterred by his cousin's hostility, was making sure he had stout friends to support him.

So Marian stood in her court finery, bewildered and uncomfortable. Matthew's choice for her of brown and gold shot silk from Damascus had been aired after all. It had been made for this occasion but she had never worn it after her marriage. She was delighted to discover this morning that it fitted as well as ever and Nan had exclaimed at its beauty as she lifted it from the dower chest where it had lain in its wrappings, smelling of rose petals and lavender. Her high hennin was a new acquisition and the frontal was trimmed with pearls and topazes. Marian had determined on the final extravagance and her father had not said her nay. A single topaz fell on a gold chain onto her gown. Her attire was simple, as became that of a woman only recently emerging from her mourning clothes, but the richness of material and elegance of styling were satisfyingly effective. She had scrutinised her young face in the mirror. For a full hour she had debated the wisdom of shaving her eyebrows as she now saw the Queen and many of her ladies had done. She had decided against it. Despite the red-gold tint of her hair, now fashionably drawn tightly back under her frontal, her brows and eyelashes were dark, the lashes touched with golden glints at the tips, noticeable only when she lowered them to veil the now familiar mutinous light in her grey eyes. It was long since she had regarded herself this critically, as personal vanity was not considered acceptable in a widow, young or otherwise, as Matthew's sister, Susanah, had so often maliciously reminded her.

She was no true beauty, being too small and slightly built to stir the senses of men whose tastes were for maturer, more stately women. Her hair was her one attraction, unusual as it was, not golden fair as the Queen's, nor yet sandy-red or deep auburn, but a colour somewhat between the two, darker than ripe corn and long and thick to the waist. She grimaced her irritation that current fashion dictated the need for it to be hidden from view, but for one or two strands on her forehead. Her features were small and well-shaped, but the mouth betrayed exceptional strength. Like her father she could hold it in a tight line of anger when the mood took her. Grey eyes were wont to be stormy and if she did not take care, the smooth line of her brow would be deeply etched with frown lines above the straight short nose. Slight as she was she carried herself well. She betrayed no hint of nervousness now as she waited for her father to return to her side.

Men and women of the court cast her curious stares. One or two women deigned to hold her in conversation for moments only. The Queen had been truly gracious, her blue eyes lazily regarding the girl but missing nothing of her youthful freshness. There was no sign among the young men round His Grace the King of Sir Ralf Compton. Just now a desire to catch a glimpse of a familiar face warred with anger at his duplicity. He had known well enough that the man who had come to her aid so speedily that night in the city had been Edward, himself. It would have been so much less of a shock had she risen from her deep curtsey to stare into those mocking eyes, had Sir Ralf prepared her.

'We are more than delighted, Sir Humphrey, to welcome you to court and to receive so charming a lady as your daughter.' Perversely he had kept her hand tightly clasped in his own strong fingers as he assisted her to rise.

'You have kept me too long without sight of her.'

Dull colour suffused Benford's neck as he murmured conventional phrases of courtesy. Full well the King knew it was no fault of his own he had been kept from court.

Edward kept her by his side to talk. 'Your husband was well known to me, mistress. No merchant in London kept finer selections of rare cloths or charged more fairly. As you have heard, perhaps, my merchants and I are on excellent terms. They have come to my assistance more than once financially, and Matthew Hurst was a man I trusted and had need to honour. It was a shock to hear of his sudden death. Yet now your mourning is over, it is to be hoped you will find cause to be merry with us here at court. Your father must not allow you to mope and wither. You are too young and too lovely for so dire a fate.'

'Your Grace is kind,' she whispered, her eyes cast down. Was he teasing her that he treated her with such marked decorum, knowing well how he had seen her dishevelled after behaving like a hoyden without due escort to chaperon her? She had made light of the incident to her father. Certainly no mention had ever been made of the brothel where she had obtained aid. Just once her grey eyes implored the King silently not to reveal more than was necessary to Sir Humphrey. His lips had twitched. He looked beyond her to the angular, forbidding form of her parent and nodded imperceptibly. Her relief was profound but she could not trust the merry Edward to keep such a jest to himself. If he talked of it to the Queen and her ladies, or over wine with his own favourites, it might yet reach the ears of her father.

She saw him now in conversation with one of the King's gentlemen. It would be impossible yet to attract his attention, but she felt forlorn and vulnerable here, conscious that all eyes were on her, and she wondered if it was her imagination that detected one or two contemptuous glances for the merchant's widow.

She was so intent that she almost cried out when her arm was touched and she swung round startled to find Sir Ralf Compton smiling at her quizzically.

'Mistress Hurst, how good it is to see you here at court.'

She was so relieved to see him that she did not greet him as frostily as she had determined.

'Sir Ralf, I had thought to see you before this.'

His dark eyes mocked at her. 'You looked for me then?'

Nettled, she lowered her eyes and twitched at the rich silk of her skirts. 'You are known to me. Naturally I looked for a familiar face.'

He nodded, unperturbed by her coolness. 'I see your father has met old companions. He will be engaged for some time. It is hot in here. Allow me to show you the river from the garden walk. The breeze will refresh you.'

She looked uncertainly towards the group round her father and Compton smiled bewitchingly. 'There will be no impropriety I assure you. Many ladies and gentlemen walk there of an evening, we shall not for one moment be out of sight of company.'

She allowed him to lead her out of the hall. He was right. The atmosphere was stifling, suffocating with the smell of rich food, wax, perfume and stale sweat. It would take time for her to become accustomed to the press of court. Outside the air was fresh, moist from the river, no more pleasantly scented for the water was stinking on hot nights such as this, but she was free of the hostile stares and felt she could breathe again.

'You were presented?'

His question reminded her of her hostility towards him.

'Indeed we were so. Sir Ralf, you were cruel not to warn me. I have never before this evening seen the King.'

'I did not warn you because I was

forbidden to do so.' His expression was more serious now. 'When Edward commands, his subjects must obey. It pleases him to tease newcomers, not least so attractive a woman as yourself. Though forbidden to speak, I was anxious to arrive earlier so that I should be present, but I was unfortunately delayed. Will you forgive me?'

His dark eyes were liquid with pleading and she laughed at his comical expression of woe.

'His Grace embarrassed me so. I . . .'

'The King delights in embarrassing females but he rarely finds them unforgiving. He is irresistible.'

'He is a golden giant of a man.'

'Aye, and a bonny fighter in the field.'

She looked up at him sharply but his lashes now veiled his eyes. 'And a hard man to cross as Warwick will find to his cost.' He frowned as she shuddered once quite violently. 'You are cold, I must return you to the hall.'

'No, please,' she checked him with a

hand on his arm. 'It is just the sudden change from the heated air of the hall or as if 'someone walked on my grave'. Do you know the expression?'

'I do, but so gloomy a thought should not be allowed to spoil so important an occasion as your first visit to court.'

She paced beside him along the path. 'I do not find it pleasurable, in truth. The company does not seem anxious to receive me.'

He gave a short laugh. 'Take no notice, mistress. Hangers-on seldom welcome any newcomer the King might favour. I, at least, welcome your arrival. I said as much before. You have had a sorrowful time this past year. Now you must put all that behind you and enjoy the delights of court. In a month or less you will be accepted. Have no fears.'

She made no answer and he turned her gently by the shoulders to face him. 'Well?'

'Unless I am commanded I shall come rarely to court. My husband was but a merchant and little thought of by those about the King.'

'The King values his merchant acquaintances.'

'So he told me.'

'And meant it, mistress.'

'And do you number city merchants among your friends, Sir Ralf?'

He hesitated only a moment. 'Until now I have not found it desirable to do so.'

She flushed hotly and he placed a hand on the tight sleeve of her gown. 'You are no inexperienced child, Mistress Hurst. I can speak plainly enough. Since our chance meeting you have been seldom from my thoughts. I would take a wife. I will speak with your father out of courtesy. Will you tell me my plea will not be entirely without hope?'

She looked away, unwilling to meet his gaze lest she give herself away so soon. 'You go too fast to market, sir.'

'But I may go?'

'That is your choice.'

He stooped and, taking one cold little hand, turned it and kissed the palm.

'Then I am not dissatisfied.' Silently they returned to the hall and Marian was relieved to see her father approach. She was suddenly weak, close to emotional tears. She withdrew her fingers from Sir Ralf's grip and went with him, glad of her father's rigid formality to give her support.

Nan Drew came immediately to disrobe her when they reached the shop. Although anxious to hear about the great occasion, she cast only one glance at her mistress and realised that her silence was more urgently needed. Now that the need for restraint was past, Marian put herself into the girl's charge as if she were a child again. Once between the sweet scented sheets she stretched out with a sigh of utter content. It was unthinkable that he should want her. She could not believe that God had given her so great a joy. She loved him. She could cry at the thought, without reason or understanding. She had loved him from the second he had passed the cold rim of the cup

65

into her hand that first night. The King had been magnificent but this man aroused strange dark longings within her. Even here in bed her cheeks burned with shame at her unbridled thoughts.

She had accepted Matthew because she must. He had been kind and benevolent, but she would have died rather than confess to her father that as a husband he was a failure. She had submitted to his half-ashamed attempts at lovemaking, and in the end he had understood her dread and released her from the need to play the wife. He had been too long without physical love. She had marvelled at his simple goodness, sorely misjudged him. Matthew had truly loved his first wife and after her death had lived a celibate existence. His appearance belied his fastidious nature. Not once had he pressed unwilling attentions on the girl who became his second wife. Though technically Marian was no longer a virgin she knew herself in fact to have been no true wife. She was barely eighteen, having married Matthew only two months past her sixteenth birthday.

Now just the sight of Ralf Compton could reduce her limbs to so weak a state she hardly expected them to support her weight. What was it in the man which made her long for his caresses, know instinctively that she would melt into his arms with the thankfulness a traveller finds at the end of some long journey, which has seemed interminable?

She had expected to remarry, had determined on such a course. Men would find her attractive enough though no longer the fresh unspoilt girl she had been. Matthew's gold would prove a compensation for her lost virginity. She was no fool. She knew that well enough, had accepted with cool-headed logic that she would find a mate who would suit her admirably. Compton, though no peer, was well-born. She recognised this instinctively, realised too that his estates might need the gold her purse could provide, but even so she had expected him to look higher for a wife. Her heart sang with joy at the prospect that he should ask for her. She was Sir Humphrey Benford's daughter, no vulgar dame from a city guild. God give her the wit, she would be such a wife to him that he would never count the cost. And if she were not granted his love? Well what of that? How many wives expected it? It would be enough to have him in the small world of her existence. He would have no cause to complain of her. If all she had was his respect, then the saints knew it was enough.

5

In the royal household Marian found one other who was not happy at court. Lady Anne Neville, daughter of the Earl of Warwick, was equally lost and uncomfortable when she journeyed to London with her mother and elder sister, Isobel, to join her stern father at his town house. She was slight and frail and her pale timidity touched a maternal cord in Marian's heart, when she saw the girl, standing, as she had done, on the fringe of company round the Queen, her eyes searching anxiously for someone whom she obviously longed to see.

Marian hesitated before thrusting herself forward. It was a month now since she had been granted a place among the Queen's ladies. She had wished to refuse the honour but Ralf laughed at her forthrightness.

'Like it or not you must accept with due gratitude, my girl. The King demands your presence at court and since you are to be Lady Compton, I'll not have you hindering my chance of favour with His Grace.'

She'd smiled back, though her mouth had twisted wryly. All she desired was to have Ralf to herself. They were betrothed, solemnly contracted in Holy Church and even now she could not believe in her happiness. Sir Humphrey had offered no objection to the match. True he had said little in Compton's favour but since the King desired it, then his Marian must wed the man. He thanked the saints she seemed besotted with the darkly handsome young courtier. Every second of each day was given to preparing for his visit, delighting in the hours of his company and in dreaming after he had left her. Sir Humphrey had cautioned them against undue haste. Marian's loss was still close and Matthew's relatives must not be allowed to think harshly of her.

Indeed it was Susanah Hurst who finally provided Marian with a suitable reason for accepting the Queen's invitation with good grace. Her sister-in-law had invaded the shop in the Chepe on hearing of Marian's intended marriage. Her disapproval hung like a pall of dun smoke over the house and shop. Apprentices avoided her glassy stare and compressed lips, and even Sir Humphrey quailed under her awe-inspiring gaze when he spoke of the match. To Marian she said nothing, but the girl was thankful to escape her presence and sought refuge at Westminster.

The Queen had received her graciously. Elizabeth Woodville was pleasant enough when not crossed. Her ladies' duties were not onerous. So long as they prepared the Queen lovingly for the day ahead, she was content to allow them freedom for the rest of it, neither did she enquire too closely into their activities. She would lounge on her daybed after the ritual of the morning toilet in all the glory of her mature beauty, drinking in the worship of the male courtiers who thronged round her in the wake of her brother, the scholarly Anthony Woodville. If the King neglected her for other beauties, she accepted the knowledge with a good-humoured shrug. He gave her all that she desired and favoured the members of her family highly. What more could she expect? He would return to her bed when it suited him. Once or twice her lovely brow creased when she thought of the son she had as yet been unable to produce for him, but even this she thought of but rarely and dismissed the problem as one that would solve itself in God's good time.

Marian would have welcomed the opportunity to serve her more arduously. Time hung on her hands. Her companion ladies, though not openly hostile, offered no friendship and more and more she found herself friendless and dispirited until Ralf came to her side and they could laugh and gossip, oblivious of everyone but themselves.

It was not to be wondered at that the unhappiness of little Anne Neville should be a bond which drew them together. Marian's half-embarrassed overtures of friendship were received with delight and she found the younger girl a more spirited companion than she had first thought. Anne's elder sister, Isobel, more outgoing in her manner, was duly judged the stronger willed of the Earl's daughters, but Marian was soon to find it was not so. Underneath the quietness and gentleness of manner, Anne could be rocklike, impossible to be moved from any fixed intention. Her natural reserve sprang more from her dislike of court company and a longing for her native Yorkshire, than a readiness to be ruled by others. She said little, but what she did say was forthright and to the point. Marian came to admire the fair girl, and pity her obvious position as pawn in her father's interests.

Soon, too, Marian came to recognise the object of her devotion. Richard of

Gloucester, the King's younger brother, had served with George of Clarence under Warwick and had learned his skill at arms at Middleham. The two had drawn together as the younger children, ignored by George and Isobel with childish, lordly disdain. It was now plain that Gloucester yearned to wed his cousin's daughter and only his brother's command stayed his hand. Once he appeared, brooding and slight, by his glorious brother's side, Anne's eyes would light up with her shy adoration. Marian was deeply touched to see the anxious glances each gave to the other and became involved later in arranging for hastily contrived meetings where they could be alone, safe from prying eyes if only for moments.

Even now she had left them together in a quiet corner of the Queen's privy garden. The Countess of Warwick was in the Queen's apartments paying a duty call. Anne had pleaded to go into the garden too with Mistress Hurst.

'The strawberries are plump and

ripe. Her Grace says we may pick one or two.'

The Countess had nodded, her thoughts on weightier matters, and also given to the problem of disguising her contempt of the Queen's slothfulness.

Anne had sped to her tryst with Gloucester while Marian had a weather eye open for others who would see the freshness of the garden after the airlessness of the rooms at Westminster. She waited for almost an hour. The sundial told her the need to remind Anne of her mother's natural suspicions. She put down her embroidery on the rustic bench where she was sitting, picked up a small wicker basket for the strawberries and sought the guilty pair.

Evidently they had hidden themselves well for she could find them neither among the strawberry patch nor in the primly bordered terraces near the river. It was clear they must be in the rose arbour. She smiled, shaking her head at the need to chide them for their rashness. She turned down the walk, the sweet scent of columbines and honeysuckle teasing her nostrils.

The Duke's voice muffled by heavy foliage told her she had been correct in her guess. Soft as it was it carried to her ears with the finality of a death knell.

'Whatever you say, sweet coz, I think she is wasted on the man. I'd wish her a fairer suitor. Compton has been a wastrel and lecher. It's unlikely he will change for her sake. Yet since 'tis Edward's command he will wed with Mistress Marian.'

'Dickon, she *loves* him. She told me so. Can you not be mistaken in your opinion of him?'

'Mistaken or no, it is plain Compton is ready enough to profit by the King's wish.'

'Marian is wealthy — that is true enough. She will not be the first at court to be wed for the contents of her dowerchest.' Anne's gentle voice carried an unaccustomed note of bitterness, 'As I know well enough to my cost. Marian is no fool. She knows Sir Ralf's estates need her gold and is glad to be able to help him in this.'

'Aye, the King thinks such a use for it more fitting than lining Sir Humphrey's purse to be used for the wrong purposes. It was for this he offered Compton an earldom to secure Mistress Hurst's fortune.'

Marian stood stock still, her fingers tightening on the handle of the wicker basket. Though she knew she should acquaint the two with the knowledge of her nearness, her legs refused to move closer or her tongue to frame the necessary words.

'You think he was unwilling, Dickon?' Anne's question sounded troubled.

'I know not, my Anne. An earldom sweetens any bitter pill. There was talk of his fondness for Blanche Willoughby, Winterton's niece, but I know naught of his true feeling. I am not in Sir Ralf's confidence, nor do I associate with those in his company. I would say nothing of this now. As you know I loathe such gossip, but I have come to know and respect Mistress Hurst. I would have for her a truer match and more worthy lord.'

Marian's unwary foot caught a pebble, causing it to jar against another and begin a small slide along the pathway. Both Gloucester and Lady Anne swung round guiltily at her approach. Anne threw a hand to her mouth, betraying her fear that her friend had heard them. Gloucester's face darkened with embarrassed colour. He rose awkwardly.

'Mistress Hurst, have we stolen too long away from company?'

She ignored his evident intention to cover up his concern for her feelings.

'Lady Anne, it has been an hour — longer. I feel we should soon return to the Queen's apartments.'

Anne came to her side and reached out for her hand. 'You heard us?'

'Yes. It was unavoidable. I'm sorry.'

'I am sorrier, lady.' Gloucester faced her squarely. 'I would not for the world have given you pain.'

'I cannot believe, My Lord of Gloucester, that you would ever make idle gossip or say anything you did not believe to be true.'

He lowered his eyes, unwilling to meet her gaze.

She continued evenly. 'Evidently you have contempt for Sir Ralf Compton.'

He moved uneasily. 'I could wish my brother to favour more worthy associates.'

Anne saw that this conversation was giving nothing but distress. 'Let us go,' she said quickly.

They left Gloucester staring miserably after them. Marian thought he had never looked so boy-like. His usually grave air gave him the appearance of being much older than his seventeen years.

As they entered the palace, Anne said timidly, 'I do not think Richard has been long enough at court to know Sir Ralf Compton well.'

'He is a good judge of character, your Richard?'

Anne's blue eyes darkened with the intensity of her distress. 'I have always thought so — but . . . '

'Say no more, my lady. It was unfortunate I overheard what was not meant for my ears.'

Anne hesitated. 'Marian, you said yourself that you know your fortune makes you a desirable match.'

'Yes.'

'Well — does this make so great a difference? You love him, do you not?'

Marian did not answer, then, as her companion touched her arm lightly, she said, 'I thought I was to marry a man who chose me for his own reasons, not on the command of the King.'

There was nothing further to say and Anne drew away towards the Queen's apartments where she knew her lady mother would be awaiting her impatiently.

It was late that evening before Marian had opportunity to speak privately with her father. She had not seen Sir Ralf during the day and was thankful for it. She would have been unwilling to meet him without anger. Doubtless pressing business kept him from court, or, she thought, with a curl of her lips, the brothel where they had first met had more urgent calls on his attention. All day she had pursued her duties as if in a dream. She told herself, almost angrily, that what the Lady Anne had said was no less than truth. She had always known why Ralf had chosen her. Why now was she so hurt by Richard of Gloucester's tactlessly uttered words? He was but a boy when all was said and done. Often she had thought that it mattered not why Ralf loved her. She would be his bride. It had been enough. Now she realised it was not so. Her betrothal was on the King's order and Ralf had tamely submitted and to make matters worse — accepted a bribe for the sacrifice of himself, the earldom of Saxby. It was not to be borne.

Why should the King want this marriage so urgently? Gloucester had spoken of her father — of the King's dislike that her fortune should pass into his keeping. He was a gambler, true. She knew that well, but in what ways should he so misuse her gold that it might harm the King's cause? It seemed unthinkable. Her mind pondered the King's reasons. If he had no love for her father, why should he so oppose her freedom of choice — for no reason except ... Angry colour suffused face and throat and she refused to consider the alternative. If the King desired her, he could not in honour command another to become her husband — and yet ... Her mind shied away from the memory of the night she had seen him first. His bold eyes had surveyed her with scant respect. *He* it was who had gone so swiftly to her aid, not Ralf. It would not be the first time a King had found a husband willing to be cuckolded for a price, in order to have a woman nearer to hand. If Ralf had agreed to so sell himself, he was lower than the meanest creature in the

Sanctuary of Westminster. To use his wife thus! It was not to be tolerated. Her father must grant her justice. She set herself to perform her duties about the Queen without sign of the hurt deep within herself. Patiently she must wait, until she could speak with her father.

He listened without comment. She had drawn him into the scant privacy of an oriel window. For the moment they were unobserved and no one near enough by to overhear. Such opportunities seldom occurred at Westminster. She shared her room with four other ladies of the Queen's household. There was no peace to be found there. She spoke softly and without choler. She must not betray herself here, in the presence of those who would carry her words to the King.

Sir Humphrey's eyes narrowed. Beyond that he gave little sign of increasing anger.

'So,' he said at last, 'the wind then sits in *that* quarter.'

'You will speak to Sir Ralf for me?'

she pleaded, swallowing her desire to speak more urgently.

His eyes widened again and he stared down at her in astonishment. '*Speak* to him? What should I say. That we are aware of his reasons? That would avail us little.'

She drew back from him, her lips parting in the suddenness of her bewilderment.

'You would not have me wed him now? You must break the contract. How can you take this so tamely? Gloucester said . . . '

'Aye, I heard you say what Gloucester said.'

'Then . . . '

'Be circumspect, girl. Do not raise your voice. Lord Hastings eyes us closely. Smile. Give the impression we are talking of other things.'

'Father . . . '

'Come, walk outside with me. We shall be less carefully observed.'

She drew a deep breath of relief. Indeed he *was* taking her words seriously. For a while she had thought he intended to brush aside her anger. He kept a hand on her arm, steadying her, forcing her to pace beside him calmly. If he felt the trembling of her body, he gave no sign. Coolly he led her to the same arbour where she had overheard Gloucester speaking with the Lady Anne, looked about him then signalled for her to seat herself.

'Now, my girl, tell me again — accurately, each word is important — exactly what Gloucester said about the King.'

Mystified she repeated them. They had seared across her soul. There was no possibility that she could have forgotten anything. His frown deepened and afterwards she waited, tersely, for his verdict.

'Do you think it true that the earldom of Saxby was the King's bribe to Sir Ralf?' She broke at last into his reverie.

'Possibly, quite probably.' His tone was testy. Compton's acquisitions did not concern him at present. He rapped an impatient hand against the wooden support of the rose arbour.

'I have not seen him today. It is fortunate since you should be the one to break the betrothal. You will do it?' She rarely stooped to plead, knowing him impervious to her wishes. Once before he had shown a deaf ear to her impassioned pleas but now he himself was involved, his honour impugned. In this, an act against the King's express command, she needed his support. He could not, *must* not refuse her.

He peered at her across the shade of the arbour. 'You talk wildly, girl. What should I say to Compton? The match is made.'

'I will not wed with him.'

His head jerked abruptly at the proud finality of her tone. 'Eh, what's this? You've changed your tune hastily it seems. Hours ago you were anxious enough to go to his bed and soon.'

She flinched at the brutality of his expression but he pressed on.

'You know well enough Compton

does not wed you for your bright eyes.'

Those eyes flashed at him now, sparkling with the explosion of her anger.

'I like not a man who acts at the King's order.'

'Pish, girl. What think you men do but act at the King's order? I tell you it is not lightly to be ignored if you're to keep your head on your shoulders.'

'Are you not furious to hear this? Doesn't it move you at all?'

'Aye, it moves me. I find the affair interesting. In spite of all, I see some good to be achieved by the situation.'

She stood up, impatient to leave his side since it was clear he had no intention of aiding her. 'I'll not wed him,' she said quietly. 'I have said it and I mean it. If you will not speak to him, I will, yes and to His Grace the King too if there is need.'

Cruelly he reached across and seized her wrist, his fingers biting into the soft flesh. 'You'll say naught without my advice, and for the present that is to act as if nothing was changed.'

She struggled to release herself, close to tears of fury. Once more he had failed her. She was determined this time no longer to be ruled by him since she now knew her happiness meant nothing to him. His desires were elsewhere. She had always suspected it, now, in a flash, she understood that he too intended to play her as a pawn in some game of power.

'I told you when you came to London this time I will wed with whom *I* wish. You will not force me.'

He flung her back against the wooden seat. 'I force you? Are you mad? The King wishes it. The *King*. His desires are not so lightly to be thrown aside. Like it or not, you will wed Ralf Compton.'

'And if I do not?' Her mouth was suddenly dry.

'There is no question of refusal. You will do it. God's teeth, why the fuss? You'll be a countess, no light accomplishment for a merchant's widow. You come not badly out of it.'

'And you?' Fiercely she reminded him of the King's intention to withdraw from him control of her fortune.

He paused and turned back to her, his lips curled back oddly as she had seen him once before. Even here in the gloom of the arbour she saw clearly the snarl of some animal which was preparing for the attack. There was the flash of teeth, then he was smiling at her normally again. He even reached down to pat at her hand in a comforting gesture, quite alien to his nature.

'I'll not come badly out of the affair, I promise you. Be sensible, Marian. The fellow is comely enough. He'll have the wit to make a pleasing groom if you handle him well. You'll say naught of this. Marry him as you intended. Show him you love him well. You did do so. You'll do so again, never fear. This is but a cut against your woman's pride, natural enough but you're no simple maid, unaware of hard facts. You know why your husband weds you.' He shrugged. 'What of it? Many maids care not so long as they wed. There is no way out of this and it's better to forget what you heard. When you've a child under your heart, you'll care not. So I tell you and I know.'

'And if I do rebel?'

Again she felt that stirring of the wild beast consciousness within him, though his smile was broad.

'It would avail you nothing. The King would take steps to force your obedience. A month in some remote border castle with Compton and what then would be your attitude? Besides,' he scratched his chin ruminatively, 'you have some thought for my life, I trust?'

'Your life?' She echoed his words almost stupidly.

'Aye, think, lass. If the King trusts me not with your gold, he'll take steps to see I don't live to use it.'

'He could not accuse you falsely.'

He shrugged again. 'You know not the world, my girl. An open accusation is not needed. A dagger in the back would suffice. Such a fate could be yours even, if your husband suspects you know his motives, therefore your best defence in the game is to act as if you are innocent of all duplicity. Compton will marry a loving wife, one who trusts him utterly. What better for our purpose?' He bent forward and drew her gently to her feet, waiting while she set her appearance to rights and quietened her trembling limbs. Her eyes searched his bland countenance in an attempt to read his intentions, but it was useless. Her thoughts raced wildly round in her brain as they recrossed the distance back to the palace entrance. What purpose had her father for Sir Ralf Compton and what indeed was to be her part in it?

6

Marian curled herself into a ball in the great bed and shut her eyes tightly against the light. Nan sounded cheerful as usual as she called from the window.

'It is sunny this morning, lady. The rain is over and the grass is so green. It's beautiful. Do you think we shall be able to go out at last?'

Unwillingly Marian uncurled and stared upwards at the dancing spot of sunlight above her head. 'Oh Nan, why did you wake me? Surely it's early yet.'

The little maid came briskly to the bedside and deftly placed the tray she carried on the chest where Marian could reach it.

'It is but two hours till noon. Lady Grace was asking for you.'

Marian thrust out her lip in an expression of sudden petulance. Did everyone in the house have to defer to

Lady Grace? Had she escaped the surveillance of one watchdog only to have the position at once filled by another? If Ralf left her here in Norfolk in this dreary waste during the icy winds and driving rains of the winter, he must expect her to spend her hours in bed. There was little else to do with the time. Since his mother disapproved so strongly, she could report to him, if and when she saw him again. Marian avoided Nan's anxious eyes as she reached for the ale tankard. She wanted little to eat though Nan had prepared the meat and new bread with her own hands, but her throat was parched.

Was it only months since Ralf had brought her to his Norfolk manor? It seemed like a century. Even those dour days under the baleful eye of Susanah Hurst had not seemed so long and dreary. To be fair she could not complain of her treatment. Ralf's mother, Lady Grace, deferred to her wishes, seemed anxious to please her, but what could one do in this wilderness where the gulls swooped over house and garden, making the air melancholy with their plaintive cries?

Had Ralf been here, she would have been content, but he was in London, supposedly in attendance on the King during the crisis. It had taken him but little time to find an excuse to return. Even after months of separation it still hurt to think of his desertion. In what had she failed him? Not by one facial muscle had she allowed him to know how much her discovery of the King's command had disturbed her. Her father had made himself very plain. To do so would be ill-advised. After due consideration she saw that. There was naught to be gained. Despite her anger she still loved Ralf. Now, after months of growing resentment, she continued to do so.

They had been married quietly as her recent bereavement behoved, but the King had been present, smiling benignly and kissing the bride with more enthusiasm than custom demanded. She had been unable to rid herself of nervousness during the ceremony. Her father's hawklike regard had not wavered. One false move on her part would have brought down the full force of his anger. As she knelt at the altar with Ralf she told herself bitterly that for the second time in less than two years she was allowing herself to be given away as a horse or dog is given. Tamely she had submitted, though she had longed to tear her hand from her husband's grasp as he stooped to place the ring on her finger and run from the chapel to sob out her despair in the privacy of her own room. Even that comfort would have been denied her, since one or other of her companions would doubtless have been there. So she had repeated docilely the words the priest had bidden her utter and had become again a wife.

She dismissed Nan, promising that she would try to eat something. She took little interest in the matter of her dress. When Nan asked what she was to lay out for the day, she shrugged and Nan turned to the dower chest and lifted out what she considered her mistress's finest gown of green velvet, trimmed with marten fur at shoulders and bosom. It was one of the collection Marian had had made for her wedding. Now she seldom wore any of them, would have existed in her mourning clothes had not Nan been determined to keep her looking her best.

'Where would you be if Sir Ralf came home unexpectedly?' she had chided.

As the girl went out, quietly closing the door, Marian ruefully considered the remark. She knew Nan had been watching anxiously as had Lady Grace for any sign of pregnancy. They had put her listlessness, her lack of appetite perhaps, to speculation about the promise of an heir. They need not have done so. Marian was quite sure that could not be the case.

She turned over now that she was alone in the room and cowered among the sheets, as if she would hide her own bitter disappointment and shame even from herself. She had failed Ralf utterly, she knew that. Even now she could hear her own cries of pain, feel the trembling of her limbs as she had withdrawn from him, terrified by the passion of his love-making. He had been at first bewildered by her reaction, later amused and finally disgusted. He had not expected a child in his arms. She had been a wife. Why then had she been unable to respond?

When the sick fear in her eyes, as he approached her the morning after she had become his bride, had told him of her dread, he had turned away impatiently. Oh, he had been courteous enough, gentle with her, but he had not taken her to his bed again. Later he had brought her to Norfolk, to bring back the colour to those faded London cheeks, he had said. She had been jubilant at his decision. Once away from court where other women were more easily at hand, he would be gentle with her again and she would prove herself worthy of his love. A second time would be her chance. She would not be foolish and betray this childish weakness which had turned him from her. But it had not proved so. Once he had established her in his manor-house, left her in his mother's charge, he had hastened back to London where he said he was needed at the King's side. Warwick could not be trusted and every Yorkist loyal to the King's cause should be close to the court of Westminster.

The house was a pleasant one, in much better condition than she had expected and not long built. Lady Grace was distant but kind enough, ready to receive her new daughter-in-law, but not one to show demonstrative affection. She was tall and stately, her dark hair like Ralf's own was only now showing threads of grey. It seemed to Marian that her lively dark eyes were constantly watching her and finding her wanting in dignity. Unlike Susanah Hurst, Grace Compton would never have demeaned herself by hectoring or shouting abuse at the younger woman. Always she greeted her with an outward show of warmth but Marian did not rid herself of a feeling that her mother-in-law was disappointed in her son's choice of bride. If only it were true, Marian told herself passionately, that I could give him an heir and soon, she would regard me with greater favour, but it was not to be. There were no signs to tell her a child would be born of their one night of true marriage. Before Lady Grace's desire could be accomplished, Ralf must return to her and she saw little hope of that at present. She had seen him only once since he left her. He had come to Compton Manor for the two days of Christmas then as hurriedly returned to court.

When Nan returned to help her dress, she was pleased to see that the girl was right. It was a fine spring day and the trees in the parkland beyond the herb garden were beginning to show traces of pale green. She flung open the window and breathed in the moist air. It had rained for so many days that the atmosphere was heavy with the wet earthy smell, which was strangely refreshing after the mustiness of her closed room.

Lady Grace looked up at her as she descended the stair. 'Good morrow, Marian. I was about to call you. There is a visitor in the hall.'

For one heart-stopping second Marian believed she was teasing her and that Ralf had come home but one glance at the older woman's face told her it was a stranger who awaited her. Grace Compton was not of a nature to play tricks on her family. There was no cause for rejoicing in the arrival of the visitor. Had it been so, she would have shown it clearly enough.

Intrigued despite her listlessness of the past days, Marian's feet carried her more swiftly towards the stone-flagged hall of the house, now rarely used, as her father's was, to entertain company or as an eating place for the household, but merely as a reception room from which other rooms led off.

The man who bowed to her as she entered was indeed strange to her. He was a big man, broad shouldered, massive chested, like the King she thought with a fleeting remembrance of the golden giant who had ordered her life. He came forward into a patch of sunlight from the window and she saw that he was young, little older than herself, with a frank open countenance, crowned by thickly waving brown hair. His voice was attractively deep, though soft, as if he had lowered it purposely to please her.

'Lady Compton, forgive me if I intrude. I bear greetings from your father. He regrets he cannot leave London at present and commends his good wishes to you. Allow me to introduce myself. I am Giles Crosby. I have recently become acquainted with your father and been of some service to him as a secretary. Since I was in

Norwich on business concerning my own family, he asked me to be the bearer of a letter for you.'

She was touched by her father's thoughtfulness. In the past he had not been wont to consider her loneliness. She smiled her gracious thanks and half turning to Lady Grace who had followed her, tentatively bade him welcome.

The older woman nodded. 'Indeed, sir, we are glad of news from London. You will eat with us?'

Giles Crosby flushed with pleasure. 'I would be honoured. Sir Humphrey bade me carry news of his daughter's state. It will please me to have some time in her company that I might report to him faithfully.'

Unaccountably Marian was pleased that today she was looking her best. It was long since she had basked in the warm glow of male admiration and she was as eager for news as Ralf's mother.

'London was quiet over Christmas. There have been no open stirrings of

Lancastrian revolt but the Earl of Warwick quarrelled with the King, it is said, during the festivities. It is true that he comes not to court now. He keeps his Countess and two daughters cloistered in the town house. It must be dull for them.'

Marian's heart bled for Anne, separated so hardly from her Richard. She asked timidly for news of her husband. Had Master Crosby seen Sir Ralf?

He had indeed and judged him in good spirits. Only a week ago he had seen him dancing a sprightly measure.

Marian declined to ask after his partner, judging it more prudent to remain uninformed.

Crosby went on to repeat what he had heard, that Sir Ralf would be My Lord Earl shortly, so high was he in royal favour, and even that His Grace the King intended a visit to this Norfolk house.

Lady Grace flushed darkly with pleasure. Marian forbore to comment. It hurt even now to think for what service her husband had gained so worthy a reward. She half listened while Crosby went on to talk of other matters.

Later, over dinner, she was pleased by the man's courtly manners. He was no fop, indeed his talk was like his countenance, direct and simple, but he paid his compliments on the house and service so ingenuously that even Lady Grace was delighted in his company. As he was staying in the neighbourhood, both women were pleased to invite him to call during the next day. Marian, at least, was relieved to know he did not intend to return to London for some days.

Next morning found her up and breakfasted early for the first time in weeks. Nan was gratified to see her mistress in such good spirits. Almost impatiently Marian awaited Master Crosby's visit and was embarrassed but overjoyed when he asked her to ride with him.

'The weather is so much improved

today and I know not the area. It would please me if you and Lady Grace were to ride forth with me, to the sea perhaps?'

Lady Grace declined. It was long since she had ridden so early in the year. The chill winds pierced through her, she said, 'No, sir, my joints would ache for days,' but her smile was genuine when she urged Marian to accompany him. 'Go, child, it will do you good. You've lingered too long indoors. William, my old groom, will go with you both, since neither of you knows the land well. Ralf would wish you to take the air on so sunny a day and in such pleasant company.'

Marian was not an accomplished horsewoman. She had ridden hardly at all during her life in London or when mourning Matthew, and her father had paid little attention to equestrian training when she was but a child in Northamptonshire, but William chose for her a gentle chestnut mare and Master Crosby's hack ambled happily beside her through the parkland and then onto the heathland near the sea. William, at the rear, kept a discreet distance.

The wind blew hard from the sea and she shivered a little as she stared over the heavy pewter mass of water. The sea birds swept round them but today their melancholy calls had no power to disturb. The Spring sun still had little strength to warm them but it twinkled and flashed over the dark sea and transformed it from a sullen monster to sparkling points of light. They quaffed ale at a small tavern, where the bush outside told them the brew was newly completed.

Giles Crosby grinned to see how her skin glowed under the chafing of sun and wind.

'You look happier, Lady Compton. I am pleased to recognise the signs.'

'You thought me in ill humour, sir, when you called yesterday?'

He corrected himself hastily. 'Nay, you wrong me, but the weather has been foul of late and I thought you must be bored in that bleak house, away from the court where you have been used to enjoy a wealth of company.'

'I miss not the company, sir.' She shook her head ruefully. 'A merchant's widow is not well received at court. Even now I fear many of my husband's acquaintances must feel that he has made a bad bargain.'

'That could never be, mistress.' Crosby was vehement and he flushed under her enquiring expression. 'I mean, lady, there must be many to envy him — even the King himself.'

'You think so?'

Crosby peered at her anxiously, puzzled by the cold note which had suddenly crept into her voice. Sensing all was not well, that somehow, unwittingly, he had spoken words to offend her, he called mine host, paid the reckoning and prepared to accompany her home.

7

During the next few days Giles Crosby was a frequent visitor to Compton Manor. Grace Compton passed no comment but she could not fail to note the pleasure Marian found in his company. She showed him the newly completed house with a sense of pride. Ralf's father had been content to live most of his life in the keep nearer the village, but the structure had long fallen into disrepair and Ralf persuaded him to begin a more comfortable modern dwelling on a rise to the east of the cluster of houses round church and keep which formed the village of Compton. The old man had been only luke-warm in enthusiasm for the scheme but had reluctantly agreed. The house was only semi-fortified. Ralf had put the men to digging drainage ditches from the marshes to form the new moat which completely surrounded the property. Twin towers supported the gatehouse which faced the drawbridge spanning the moat, and led into the inner courtyard. Archery slits were provided in the turret towers at each corner of the house, and the newel stairs led up from the towers to the battlemented walks above, but inside the house was more pleasant than Marian could have imagined. Private bedchambers were provided not only for the knight and his bride but for all guests and the parlours and dining room gave privacy not previously provided in the old keep. Lady Grace seemed satisfied though there was yet much to be done. Ralf planned a mellow brick wall round the house, formal gardens, finer stables and outbuildings. No wonder he required money, but Marian realised with a relieved sigh that the estate was not impoverished as she had supposed.

Giles Crosby accompanied her on her habitual walks round the house.

Dutifully he echoed her words of gratification. It *was* a fine house. There was none finer in the neighbourhood and one thing only remained to cloud her acceptance of it. Since there was yet much remaining to complete the building, why had Ralf absented himself at a time when he should be supervising the workmen? He did not now lack for funds, for her coffers were open to him.

Despite her irritation, Marian was now feeling much happier. No longer did she lounge in her chamber till the sun was almost overhead. Eagerly she rose and breakfasted with Lady Grace then was out of doors and about her work of supervising the maidservants. Nan muttered beneath her breath when Marian insisted on wearing her finest gowns. Since it was usual for Master Crosby to call, her mistress was determined to look her best on all occasions.

For two or three days the weather worsened and rain poured down in a steady veil. Marian peered dispiritedly through the casements onto a sodden landscape and despaired of riding out on the jaunts she had now begun to enjoy.

The fourth day dawned clear. The sun was still watery but when Giles Crosby arrived she greeted him with delight.

'Giles, it is good to see you. I quite thought the rain would never stop and we should have to take to the ark or some like vessel.'

He laughed but she was quick to note that despite his wish to be pleasant for her sake he was unusually quiet.

'Giles, what is it? Have you had bad news?'

He shook his head. 'No news at all. That is the worst of it. I must go back to London tomorrow.'

'Oh.'

He seized on her little *moue* of distress. 'I cannot regret that the news displeases you, although it causes you unhappiness.'

'We seldom see visitors. I have come

to look forward to our outings, but I realise I have been selfish. You must be anxious to get back to court. I will write to my father if you will carry the letter for me.'

'Indeed I will, lady, but since it is our last day will you ride out with me? True, it is still not warm, I fear, but the sun shines and it is dry enough.'

She went into the solar to write her news for her father. There was little to say since life had been quiet of late. She informed him of the improvements being completed at the house and bade him carry her greeting to her husband, then, hastily sealing the missive, she hastened above stairs to don more suitable clothes for riding.

They were both rather subdued during the ride. Marian knew she would miss this personable young man greatly. He was considerate and gentle. She liked his grave demeanour and the occasional quips which lightened the gravity of his habitual manner. His visits had brought her out of her despondency, and, though grateful, she was careful not to give him any encouragement. Though he said naught that could offend her, she felt his growing interest and as they neared the Manor at the end of the ride she could not repress a faint tremor of relief that he would not come again to Compton or at least for so long that Ralf would surely have returned to her.

She turned away from Master Crosby as a faint flush dyed her cheeks at thought of her husband. Indeed she had thought of him rarely during this last week. William had kept a discreet distance from them as he had done on all their rides and he rode up now to take their horses when Master Crosby dismounted and lifted her from the saddle.

'You will take wine with us and the letter is in the solar. Remember you promised to carry it.'

He bowed gravely. 'I have not forgotten.'

Though dry the day had proved cold

and Marian led the way quickly into the solar, anxious to warm her hands at the blaze in the great open fireplace. Impatiently she thrust back her hood and called for Nan to attend her.

Lady Grace was seated near the fire. Marian was surprised to see they had another visitor, for a man stood behind her partly in the shadow, his back turned from her in the action of pouring wine. Her ladyship looked up quickly at Marian's entrance and the man turned at once.

'Ralf.' The cry burst from her lips and she stopped dead, half embarrassed, half bewildered by her first sight of him.

Ignoring her obviously shocked reception of him, he calmly gave the wine goblet to his mother and came towards her and taking her hands, turned them palm upwards as he always did and raised them to his lips.

'Forgive me, my wife, that I did not send ahead to warn you of my coming, but the storms have been so bad that I could not send out a dog in such weather, and today I was in haste to greet you after this long time of parting.'

His dark eyes gazed beyond her to Giles Crosby standing hesitant in the doorway.

Marian stammered out an introduction. 'Master Giles Crosby, Ralf, my father's secretary. He brought greetings from London for me and is to carry my letter in return.'

Crosby was brick red with embarrassment, obviously unused to the company of distinguished men of the court. He bowed low, uttering one or two almost unintelligible words of polite greeting.

'You are welcome, Master Crosby. 'Tis hoped my wife and mother have made you comfortable on your visits. Do you stay long in Norfolk?'

'Alas, I start for London tomorrow, Sir Ralf.'

Compton raised his brows in polite regret. 'You will dine with us, perhaps.'

Crosby demurred. 'If you will excuse me, Sir Ralf, I have preparations to make . . . '

'Of course.' Ralf's smile was sincere. While Marian hurried to find her sealed letter, he plied their guest with wine. Surprisingly the package did not appear to be on the small table where she had left it. She gave a quick look round the room, shaking her head as Lady Grace rose as if to assist her in her search. She crossed to her and whispered, 'I have mislaid my letter. Perhaps I took it to my chamber when I changed. I think not but it is possible.'

Lady Grace frowned. 'I did not see a letter. One of the servants may have moved it. They were cleaning in here an hour or so ago.'

'No matter.' Marian hurried out of the room. Sir Ralf was still engaged with his visitor. He cast her an enquiring looked over his shoulder then returned his attention to Crosby.

It was not in her chamber. Marian bit her lip in uncertainty. Surely it could not have been destroyed. It was so obviously newly written and bore her father's name. No servant would have dispensed with it. Most were unable to read but they would have questioned Lady Grace about it or replaced it where it had lain. It was a mystery. Nan was nowhere to be seen. She might have kept the letter safe somewhere from prying eyes. She must wait and ask the girl later. It was irritating, to say the least. There would be few opportunities to send a messenger to her father.

As she re-entered the solar, she heard Ralf's voice. 'His Grace should be here tomorrow or the day after. His visit will honour our house, short though it must be. He journeys to Norwich by the end of the week. It has irritated me to be delayed. I had hoped to make adequate preparation . . . '

Marian's face paled. She paused in the doorway her question cutting off his sentence.

'The King, here — at Compton?'

Ralf turned to her, his face alight

with the pleasure of his news. 'I know you will have wished for longer time to prepare. However it cannot be helped. Yes, my love, he comes soon now. I rode ahead to bear the news.'

'But why does he come here? It is not possible. The house is small. His household cannot be accommodated.'

Lady Grace rose, her expression showing her utter astonishment at Marian's reaction. Ralf did not wait for her to speak. His interruption cut like a lash, 'God save us, madam, do you question the King's intention? I know womanly fears at such times. You fear the house will be unready. Edward will know that well enough. He has spoken of his desire to see you again. Be not foolish, Marian. This house-wifely attitude is unseemly.'

She swallowed hard, thrusting aside betraying words which might have been uttered in her first shock. He had covered her tactless utterance, but his eyes were hard and she knew he had recognised her repugnance to meet the

King. Crosby's eyes had widened at their exchange. He moved a trifle uncomfortably.

'The house is in excellent state, lady. I am sure you have no cause to fear royal displeasure.'

'No — I am sure — that is . . . ' She came to her husband's side as anxious as he now to make excuses for the words which should never have been spoken in company. Her little laugh sounded to her own ears, brittle, unreal.

'His Grace will not expect the luxuries of Westminster, here at Compton, and yet my first thought is that we cannot please him and — well, I am sure arrangements can be made for his reception, hurried though they must be.' She averted her eyes from Ralf's hard gaze. 'I am sorry, Master Crosby. The letter does not come to hand. I cannot ask you to wait longer. If I find it, I will send it to your lodging early tomorrow. I thank you for all your past kindnesses. Greet my father for me and say I will write later, if you are without the package when you reach London.'

He bowed. 'I understand you will be in a flurry of activity here. I will explain to Sir Humphrey. Now I will leave you since I must be off early tomorrow and I know how anxious you will be to discuss urgent matters with Sir Ralf.'

Ralf went with him to the courtyard to bid him Godspeed. Marian ignored her mother-in-law's puzzled expression. She went to the fire, ostensibly to warm her hands but inwardly to compose her features before Ralf returned. In his eyes she had glimpsed signs that a reckoning would be demanded of her later.

8

Marian dismissed Nan after undressing and sat for a while on the heavy oaken chest by the window. She was unwilling to climb into bed and the chamber seemed suddenly airless. She pushed open the casement and peered down over the moat, abruptly pulling her furred bed-gown closer round her as a man moved nearer to the house from the garden. Seeing the glow of candle-light, he glanced upwards before entering the main door. It was Simon Wentworth. She drew the casement window closed with a bang. The boy had always disturbed her. Contempt for her was apparent in his light eyes. She regretted her earlier spoken hasty words which the boy had overheard. He had been present behind Sir Ralf when he had informed her of the King's intended visit. Ralf would not be pleased at one more witness to her indiscretion. Her cheeks burned at thought of her husband's anger.

He had spoken to her little during the evening. Lady Grace had made efforts to hide the tension between them. She had asked after former acquaintances now in London. Ralf had answered civilly enough but it was clear he was in no mood for gossip. Simon Wentworth had been silently attentive behind his chair, his expression faintly disapproving of the many times he was ordered to refill his master's cup. Undoubtedly Ralf had drunk deep and Marian was fearful of his dealings with her. She could not content herself with the thought that the wine he had imbibed would render him sleepy. When she had risen from her chair and required permission to retire, he had been coldly formal, but there was no trace of drunkenness in his voice or movement. No, Ralf was in full possession of his faculties. She could not hope to avoid a reckoning soon.

She stirred unhappily as she heard his steps ascending the stair and his dismissal of his squire. Suddenly the great bed offered a refuge and she ran forward and cowered among the silken coverings, as if they offered some protection.

He paused in the doorway and stared across the room at his wife still clutching at the furred collar of her robe. He made no comment but went aside to the curtained alcove which served him as a dressing room. While he was turned from her, she slipped clear of her bed-robe and draping it at the foot of the bed, drew up the silken covers once more. She had no wish to appear ridiculous, refusing to dispense with her gown in the presence of her own husband. He would judge her truly afraid of him.

'Well,' he said at last, as he came to her side, his own bed-robe drawn tight round his lean figure, 'it seems we have privacy to discuss our problems.'

Her grey eyes widened at his curt

tone but she thrust out her chin courageously. 'You take me to task for my dislike of the King's visit?'

'I challenge your foolishness in speaking so openly. God's teeth, woman, it is the King you speak of so slightingly.'

'You took me by surprise. I should not have spoken so before Master Crosby.' She faltered, dropping her eyes before his angry stare and plucking nervously at the linen sheet. 'You are not satisfied perhaps as to his reasons for being here. He . . .'

He cut her short peremptorily. 'Master Crosby does not concern us. If he is your father's secretary then it is likely he visit here. Think you I care for that? I trust you, madam.'

Perversely she was not relieved by his summary dismissal of Giles Crosby's presence. The man was young, personable. It seemed added fire to her hurt that her husband seemed to fear no rivalry from that quarter. Did Ralf hold her in so little respect?

'He has been kind and attentive. He

would not have been present at our meeting but for the letter he promised to carry to my father.'

He waved his hand in irritation as he sat down at the foot of the bed. 'Yes, you said as much but it is of the King we are speaking.'

'You are over-anxious for this visit.'

He frowned. 'He honours us.'

'He has honoured many men — for a price,' she flashed at him.

His frown deepened. 'What talk is this? We all know His Grace is no saint. England needs a soldier, not a monk, like poor King Harry, God bless him. Of course I'm glad he favours me.'

'With an earldom?'

One dark eyebrow lifted and his expression grew wary. 'So Crosby told you that?'

'Why should you think it was Giles?'

He shrugged. 'Who else recently came from the court? Aye, His Grace has so promised. I had not thought to find you so ungrateful.'

'For what services — or do I need to

ask?' Her tone was so cutting that he turned full towards her and leaned forward to peer into her angry little countenance.

'So — you hold your father's views after all. You are in truth Benford's daughter. I had not thought it. Well, I'll allow you to have your own leanings, but you'll keep a still tongue before His Grace. Hear me well.'

'And if I do not?'

He caught one hand in his grasp and squeezed it so that she caught back a cry of pain. 'I shall remind you of your wifely duty — obedience to your husband, madam, and with a switch if necessary.'

Angrily, she clawed at her imprisoned hand, striking at it as he continued to hold it fast. 'Whatever you do to me, I'll not surrender myself to the King. My father schooled me when he wanted me to marry Matthew. I gave way then, I'll not do so again. I'll not be the price you pay for the King's favour.'

An oath passed his lips she thought

never to hear from him. He released his hold on her hand, leaned forward and took her shoulders and shook her until her teeth rattled.

'By the saints, madam, never speak so to me again. Are you mad?'

Sobbing with fear and fury she fought to regain her composure though the violence of his jerks had caused her to bite her tongue and the salt taste of blood filled her mouth.

'You married me at his command. I know it. Do not deny it. Now he comes here because he thinks you will be generous. I'll not do it, Ralf, if you threaten to kill me.'

'Generous — with you?' He released one shoulder to tilt her face towards him. She was beside herself and had not yet realised the anger had left his tone and he was smiling at her. 'Look at me, Marian. Tell me truly. Is that what you thought, the King comes to Compton for love of you?'

His mirth brought angry, embarrassed tears to her eyes. 'Is not that why . . . '

'Wench, you think too highly of your charms. Nay,' he checked her, chuckling, as she attempted to lunge out at him with one close-balled fist, 'I will not test you further. If the King does not find you lovely, he is a fool indeed — but as to why he comes to Compton, I regret to disillusion you, sweeting, but not to take my wife to bed. He would have to deal with me first.'

She lowered her head and her bright hair fell forward and covered her face, now scarlet with shame.

'Come, Marian — is it such a disappointment? Let me give a sop to your hurt pride and tell you how anxious I was to take you from his presence, that first time when he came to your assistance.'

'Forgive me.' Her voice was muffled and he bent close to hear her words. 'I had thought . . . '

'Just what *did* you think, my sweet?'

'You — you left me so suddenly. I thought . . . ' she floundered helplessly, 'it seemed that you consummated our marriage because you must, then you returned to the King's side. At first I feared I had disappointed you, then I thought the King had so commanded it — and . . . '

Over her bent head his eyes grew grave. 'Marian, my heart, listen to me. I left you for very shame that I had understood you so little and treated you with scant patience. You had been a wife, and I expected . . . ' He broke off with a shrug. 'No matter. I was horrified at your fear of me and had not the grace to face it out. It is true Edward needed me in London and it was good excuse for me to be gone and give you time to prepare. I had not thought to take a child to my bed.'

'Then you *are* disappointed?' She lifted her head and faced him directly.

'No, Marian, truly. You will learn and I have still to teach you. That, I should have realised from the first.'

'Oh, Ralf, Ralf, I . . . ' She turned away, horrified now that he should read in her face her hopeless love for him and the relief his words had granted her. She *did* believe him, perhaps because she longed to. If he would give her part of himself, her prayers would be granted. That was all she asked. His reasons for obeying the King's commands no longer concerned her. Had he been so base as to marry his master's paramour, however great the reward, she could not have borne it.

Gently he turned her back to face him, smiling into her tear-streaked face. 'Look at me. I feared my neglect might inspire wifely chiding, never this. Tell me you are glad to see me home.'

She swallowed and opened her lips to reply but the words were never uttered for his lips closed firmly on hers and she was lost to all caution or restraint.

Lying clasped in his arms, she stared at the square of light which was the window casement. Already the darkness in the room was turning grey. Ralf slept evenly but she was wakeful. She loved him too much even now to delight in his nearness. Her cheeks burned at the shameless way in which she had surrendered to his need. Her own, starved so long for sight of him and tortured by growing doubt, had been as great and she had allowed herself to believe his whispered endearments as he wooed her body to respond to his.

He stirred and, reaching out, drew her yet more close, his teeth biting gently at her ear as she turned away her head in mock anger.

'Play not the virtuous woman with me, wench,' he said mockingly. 'It is too late for such maidenly deceits — far too late.'

Her laughter bubbled forth in spite of herself and she placed two fingers restrainingly on his lips, feeling each loved feature of his face in the darkness.

'Well, strumpet, are you satisfied your husband loves you?'

'Do I have to answer?' Her response was sleepy, husky with contentment.

'Indeed you do.'

'I love you, Ralf. If you care for me a little, it is enough.'

'Such wifely obedience. I have a pearl indeed.'

'In a golden setting.' The moment the words slipped out she could have bitten out her tongue sooner than utter them.

He released her and sat up. She could see his torso clearly, the shoulders limned against the light from the window.

'So the thought rankles. I had hoped you would forget it, though God knows you have a right to remind me.'

'My father married me to Matthew for the gold, the thought rankled then. I was sold to obtain it. Now I am chosen because I possess it. Ralf, it means nothing to me. It is yours and I am glad to give it — only . . . '

'Only?'

'Gloucester spoke of the King's command. I wondered . . . '

'So it was Gloucester. The boy distrusts me. I am sorry for that, since I would have his good will.' He sighed. 'Aye, the King was anxious that your gold should not be used by your father in the wrong cause.'

'He spoke to me of this. I do not understand, Ralf.'

'Your father leans to Lancaster. It is that the King fears.'

'But Lancaster is a lost cause.'

'Is it so?' His tone was musing.

'Ralf, there will be no further wars?'

'Warwick is dissatisfied. He has left England. The King fears he courts the favour of Queen Margaret. For this reason he comes to Norfolk to borrow what he can from wealthy merchants in Norwich.'

'But Margaret will never accept Warwick, not after Mortimer's Cross. He is related to Edward . . . '

'You sound shocked, my sweet. You will learn how easily father turns against son and brother against brother. Already we have evidence of that. Clarence had forsaken the King. There is talk he will wed Isobel Neville in the teeth of his brother's displeasure.'

She was silent, her thoughts turning to Anne Neville, the girl who had been very close to her during those friendless days in London. Giles Crosby had spoken of the way her father had kept her from court. If Anne's sister were to wed George of Clarence, what of Anne's own feeling for Richard of Gloucester? Ralf leaned over her, twisting a red-gold curl tightly round his finger.

'You fear for your father?'

'No.' She checked herself abruptly. Indeed it was unfilial to be so unconcerned about her father's motives. 'At least, I was in a way. I was thinking of others.'

'Oh?'

She laughed. 'I thought you were not jealous, my husband. You instantly dismissed Master Crosby as of no importance.'

In the strengthening light she saw his brow wrinkle in mock alarm. 'Indeed I am beginning to feel that I was unwise in so doing. I find you so improved in the art of love . . . '

He broke off with a sudden crow of pain as she pummelled at his belly as he lay beside her. He was winded with his laughter. 'My darling, I cry your mercy, but you seem determined to make me suspicious.'

'Well,' her eyes glinted with mischief, 'it is not good for a husband to be so complacent.'

Then he seized her in his arms, despite her cries of protest, and she forgot Giles Crosby and her father, the King and Anne Neville, while she gave way to his love-making. Later, as light flooded into the room, her lips curled wryly into a half smile when she thought how belated was their rising. There was much indeed to be done and the King expected at any time. She stirred her sleeping husband and bent to kiss his shoulder while he lazily rolled over, then expertly moved clear. No, decidedly, she must allow no more love-making if she was to be a hostess worthy of His Grace.

9

The King rode into Compton as dusk was falling and brands flared into life in the courtyard bringing into sharp relief the rich colours of his brightly apparelled retinue, touching cloth of gold, scarlet velvet, marten fur and the heraldic caparisoning of their varied mounts. Ralf hurried to receive His Grace with Marian by his side and Lady Grace waited discreetly by the main door near the gatetower. The King was in good humour, punching Ralf affectionately on the shoulder and bending to give Marian a great smacking kiss full on her lips.

'I vow, Ralf, your wife grows lovelier — likely so, now she has discarded that crow-like apparel.'

'We are honoured to greet Your Grace and trust you had a pleasant journey.' Ralf bowed, his eyes flickering to the slim, dark-haired figure who dismounted and walked, with the faintest trace of a limp, to the King's side. 'You too are welcome to Compton, My Lord of Gloucester.'

The Duke's grey-green eyes surveyed him somewhat coldly. He bowed his head a trifle in acceptance of the greeting, then his expression brightened at sight of Marian. She curtseyed her greeting and he stooped to kiss her hand.

The King surveyed the frontage of the house, nodding his approval. ''Tis a fair dwelling, Ralf. You can be proud of it.'

'There is still much to be done, sire, but I think you will find your apartment comfortable and there is good accommodation for your company. My Lord of Gloucester, and you, Lord Hastings, will find rooms prepared.'

Will Hastings came up to join his greeting to that of the royal brothers. He was a handsome, pleasant mannered gentleman, Marian knew well from her days at court. Lord Rivers, apparently, had stayed with the Queen in London.

A late dinner was served to the King and his intimates in the new dining hall. The King ate well and drank deep, entertaining Sir Ralf on his right, Marian on his left and Lady Grace opposite, to whom he paid such fulsome compliments that her pale cheeks flushed with pleasure. The Duke of Gloucester sat quietly on Marian's left with Lord Hastings next to him. The Lord Chamberlain was a courtly companion. He leaned forward slightly to speak to Marian across his royal neighbour. Despite the lateness of the hour when they rose from the meal, the King asked to be shown the interior of the new house and Ralf at once complied, ordering Simon Wentworth to light their way with a flaming torch. Lady Grace remained in the solar with My Lord Hastings and Duke Richard implied that he would wish to follow the King if Marian would be his guide.

After a while they were able to linger some way behind and Marian was at liberty to speak of the Lady Anne.

'I've seen nothing of her in months,' he said softly. 'My Lord of Warwick is in Calais. He is, of course, warden of the ports and has charge of Calais. My brother, George of Clarence, has joined him.'

'I heard of it. I am sorry you are separated . . . ' Marian broke off, embarrassed.

He nodded. 'And you, Lady Marian. Can it be that you are happier than I gave you cause to believe?'

She lowered her head. 'Yes, my lord. I am content.'

'God be thanked. I have prayed for such a state of affairs. You were a good friend to my Anne,' he said gently.

Marian hesitated to mention gossip she had heard from both Giles Crosby and Ralf. 'My Lord Duke, do you think there is cause for concern? Will the Earl return to his allegiance? I heard it said that he turns to Lancaster.'

'Aye, he seeks Margaret.'

He turned in the torchlight to see shocked bewilderment on her face. 'I cannot blame him. Edward has treated him badly. My cousin is ambitious. It would have been wiser to have favoured him, openly at least. I speak honestly, perhaps indiscreetly, mistress, but then I take leave to trust to my judgment of you.'

'It will come to war?'

He shrugged. 'Who knows? I cannot doubt it. Edward cares not. He thrives on battles.'

'But the Lady Anne — and you?'

He had turned his head but she read the bitterness in the tone of his voice. 'Love is not termed necessary for the happiness of princes. My brother George weds where he wishes. Isobel Neville is his chosen bride while I — I remember my motto 'Loyalty binds me'. I cannot disobey Edward, not now, when he has need of me. It is a point of honour. York comes first, my needs are secondary.

Anne knows that well enough.'

Simon Wentworth had lit one of the brands in a sconce on the wall of the corridor. She saw by its light how grave and stern he looked, then he smiled. She had seen this rare smile of his when he'd been with Anne and her own heart was touched. She longed that this stern young man would grant Ralf his approval and trust and she knew now why Ralf was concerned that the younger prince had no love for him.

'Lady Marian, we talk too seriously. I am here in your house as a guest and have no right to sadden you with my fears. God knows you dealt kindly with Anne. When affairs are normal, we shall both know how formally to thank you.'

'There will never be need for that, Duke Richard,' she said quietly.

The King called from ahead and there was no more opportunity to talk.

The need to wait on the King brought Marian to rise early. Ralf sleepily complained but His Grace had indicated that he would wish to ride over the estate if the morning was fine and she was anxious to wait upon him at breakfast. Ralf dressed and made a hasty meal, then hurried to the stables to see that all was in readiness. It was a golden day, almost balmy, the wind light and though there was a cold snap still in the air, the sun dispelled its chill and the royal party moved to the courtyard, enthusiastic for the early ride.

Marian chivied the servants about their duties and hastily prepared a stirrup cup for the King, calling to Simon to bring one to the courtyard for My Lord of Gloucester. She stopped short in the doorway at the sight of Giles Crosby crossing the drawbridge. One of the King's men had challenged him and apparently granted permission for him to proceed. He was obviously overcome with embarrassment at sight of the royal company.

Marian swallowed her irritation at his intrusion at so inconvenient a time and placed down the wine goblet for a

142

moment on the oaken chest in the hall.

'Master Crosby, please come in. You are welcome. As you see, you find us busy, but do not concern yourself. I had not hoped to see you again so soon. I thought you on the way to London by now.'

He smiled his relief at her welcome. 'I had not guessed the King would be here so soon. I was delayed. A cousin came to stay. We had not seen one another in years and I spent an extra day in his company. It occurred to me that you might now have found the letter, but I see I shall incommode you at this time.'

'No, I have not done so, but I penned another, I thought one of the King's men might carry. It is very brief but tells my father I am well and happy. Since you will be in London more quickly I should be grateful if you would carry it for me. Will you wait but a moment while I go to my chamber for it? Simon,' she called imperatively, 'go to the courtyard with the wine. Lady

Grace is busy in hall. I will join you in a moment with the King's cup.'

The squire cast Giles Crosby a curious look then with his accustomed half-sullen shrug of acquiescence he moved to obey her.

Marian glanced hurriedly into the outer courtyard. The King was not yet mounted. He was talking with Gloucester, his arm affectionately thrown round his brother's shoulder. He was gesticulating towards the moat. She still had time to fetch the letter for Giles. She took the newel stairs at a run and almost collided with Nan, who was descending. The letter was quickly found and she sped back to the entrance hall, excusing herself to Giles Crosby that she had little time to talk with him.

'You will forgive me. I take the wine cup to His Grace.'

'Of course, Lady Marian, it was kind of you to receive me. In any case I am in haste, having delayed a whole day.' He thrust her letter into the purse at his

144

belt, bowed and hurried out to take his horse from the waiting groom. She waved her goodbye and he called for his good wishes to be offered to Sir Ralf and Lady Grace. Relieved, she watched him ride over the drawbridge and turned back to her duties.

The King was now in the saddle, Duke Richard also, now spurring his own mount to his brother's side. Lord Hastings had drunk deep the previous night, as had the King, but unlike his royal master, was looking pale and wan in the sunlight. He had refused to break his fast in hall with the others but was now drinking thankfully from the cup Simon Wentworth held. The King jovially chided him for carrying his wine ill.

'Come, Will, what do they say, it is good to bind a bite wound with a hair from the dog which bit you? The wine will fortify you, my poor friend, and the sea air blow away the headache.'

Hastings grinned in answer. 'I would I had a harder head, like you, Your Grace.'

The King's booming laughter carried to Ralf as he came sweating from the stables to reach towards his own mount held ready for him by his groom, William. Seeing Marian approach with the wine, the King leaned down to take the cup from her.

'My thanks, Lady Marian, it is hard to refuse wine from so gracious and lovely a hand, but I have eaten and drunk well in hall. I believe your lord has more need of this than I.' He sidled his mount towards that of Ralf and offered the silver cup. 'Drink up, Ralf my lad. I think you've earned this.'

Ralf drained it gratefully and returned it to his wife.

'We shall be back at noon or soon after. Tell my lady mother to prepare.'

'All will be well, I promise.' She smiled at him, anxious to convince him of her worth as chatelaine. 'A pleasant ride, Your Grace.' She lifted her hand in farewell as the King nodded, called to the company and spurred ahead across the drawbridge.

Lady Grace expressed relief when Marian returned with the news that the royal party had set off in good time. Honour or no to have the King present at Compton, it meant hard work for every soul in the Manor, while both women were hard put to it to visit all parts of the house and give instructions. Marian left the jurisdiction of the kitchens in the capable hands of her mother-in-law and herself patrolled the apartments of the house to see that all was spick and span for the King's return. As Lady Grace had remarked ruefully, it would have been simpler if they had had more direct warning and time to replace one or two worn tapestries which had come from the old keep and to sweep out the old rushes everywhere and lay fresh ones. Fortunately in the chambers where the King and Duke had lain, carpets had replaced rushes, and though Lady Grace had originally thought them a sad extravagance on Ralf's part, she was thankful now, since she could be proud of the two rooms, bright with log fires and the jewel bright colours of carpets and arras.

Emerging from the King's chamber after supervising its sweeping and dusting, Marian placed a hand against her aching back. She determined to go to the buttery and have a tankard of cool ale pulled for her. As she crossed the courtyard to visit the outbuilding, she heard the sound of return. Puzzled she ran across the drawbridge to scan the road. Surely it was early yet, but no other but a great company of riders such as the King's retinue could have made such a thunder of hoof beats or raise such a pother of dust. It was so, she could see the King, resplendent in scarlet velvet doublet, in the lead, and the younger Duke in more sober dark green, his fur-lined cloak flying outwards in his haste.

Obviously something was wrong. Had there been an accident? Frightened, Marian waited tense by the gate until the group clattered into the court-yard. Both King and Duke seemed safe enough — but where was Ralf? There was Lord Hastings leading another horse and Simon Wentworth — but Ralf? The King pulled his mount up sharply and turned to assist Hastings. He saw her stagger towards him and spoke briefly over his shoulder.

'Sir Ralf has been taken ill, Mistress Marian. Summon the nearest physician.'

His usually genial expression was pale and shocked and she gave a sudden sob as Duke Richard and Lord Hastings assisted Ralf from the saddle. Horrified, she saw he was too weak to stand and hung limply in the arms of the two men.

'Ralf, my God, what is wrong?' She appealed to the King. 'What happened, sire? Did he fall? How serious is it?'

The King placed a restraining hand on her arm. 'Misress, I realise your alarm. I feel deeply for you, believe me. Let us first get Sir Ralf to his chamber and make him comfortable in his bed.'

Simon Wentworth came at his urgent summons and led the way to Sir Ralf's chamber. Marian tried to follow but the King held her back.

'One moment, lady.' He called a frightened groom to his side. 'Off with you, man, to the village and summon a physician, an apothecary, if a doctor is not to be had, but in haste. Do you hear me. Tell him Sir Ralf is in pain.'

'Aye, sir.' The man flung himself into the saddle of a horse vacated by one of the King's gentlemen and rode off at a gallop. 'Now, lady,' the King said quietly, 'has Sir Ralf seemed ill earlier today? Did he complain of stomach cramp or nausea and subdue the symptoms in our presence?'

'Pains? Ralf? No.' Marian felt her knees go weak. 'He said naught to me today or yesterday, sire. He was well. I'm sure of it.'

The King kept a steady hand on her arm as she jerked forward, anxious to follow her husband. 'Steady now, lass. Likely it is colic, or some inner chill.

The weather was bad when he set out for Compton. The onset of the attack was sudden. Let us see what Lady Grace has to say. She may know of previous attacks.'

But Lady Grace was as bewildered as their guests. She had come hurriedly to her son's chamber when she heard the news and now the King dismissed all but Marian and Ralf's mother with Nan to assist them, and he himself with Gloucester and Hastings went to the solar to await the arrival of the doctor.

Ralf looked white and sick and was obviously in great pain. He clutched at his belly and retched weakly while his mother held a basin to his lips. Nan ran, white-faced, for warm water and towels and Marian bathed his face and temples, unlaced his shirt front and bathed his chest.

'It's — all right, sweeting,' he gasped between bouts of pain, 'something I ate, though God knows what. I'll be better soon when I empty my stomach. Leave me, lass.'

Gently she soothed him. 'We'll do no such thing. Lie quiet now till the doctor comes.'

His protests against the summoning of the physician were interrupted by another bout of tearing pain which seemed to tear his vitals in two. He gave a great oath and vomited into the basin held by his mother.

She seemed very calm, saying little, though her hands shook. Her eyes mutely told Marian that this sickness was as unusual as it was unexpected. Marian was terrified. She strove to speak without panic but her limbs felt like water and she had to fight to stay on her feet. Her body was drenched in the icy sweat of fear, but resolutely she supported Ralf back against the pillows, her heart wrung with pity as almost at once he doubled up again in agony and was sick once more in the basin.

'This will weaken him so,' she said anxiously. 'When will the doctor come? Please God let him be found quickly.'

As there was no physician nearer

than King's Lynn, a distance of twenty miles or more, the groom returned with an apothecary from the nearby market town. He was tall and thin as a lath, dressed from head to foot in rusty black. He listened to Marian's explanation of the symptoms, which she told him outside the door. He nodded sagely and entered. Ralf was almost semi-conscious by this time. He could no longer vomit but he was still racked with pain and retching weakly from time to time. The apothecary stood at the foot of the bed, surveying him through narrowed lids, then he approached, placed one hand on the sick man's forehead and the other on his wrist. Ralf stirred but lapsed off again into the half stupor and the apothecary turned back one eye-lid gently.

'He has eaten naught but what you all had?' he questioned abruptly.

Marian shook her head. 'He was well enough last night. He ate new bread and meats in the hall as we all did and drank the wine in the courtyard.'

'Wine, you say?' He looked at her sharply.

'I carried a stirrup cup to the King and all the nobles who went with him drank from the same wine.'

'Hm.'

'Can you help him?' Desperation made Marian's voice sharp.

'He is gravely ill, in a high fever and exhausted from the sickness. From the way his body doubles up, I'd say his bowels were on fire. I'll do what I can.'

He opened the leathern satchel he carried and withdrew various phials and bowls. 'Later I'll bleed him to allay the fever, but not yet. First I will try to ease the pain.'

He asked for boiled water into which he dropped fine grey powder then, as Lady Grace lifted Ralf's shoulders, he raised the bowl of liquid to his lips. Marian watched anxiously as Ralf made feeble efforts to swallow at his mother's coaxing and at last downed the liquid. Her heart was wrung with pity at his childish gesture of distaste, then he fell back again like a tired child. The apothecary waited, his hand occasionally raised to his patient's brow. It was clear that the drug was taking effect. Still Ralf writhed under the fur coverings the apothecary had ordered to sweat the fever from him, but at last he seemed quieter and the apothecary nodded and indicated that Marian should go outside the door with him.

'He will sleep for a while. The pain is easier. Let him rest.' Lady Grace had remained behind. Marian led the man into the solar.

The King was pacing its length as they entered and he stopped and waited for a verdict. Behind him Marian could see the grave faces of Lord Hastings, Richard of Gloucester and the squire, Simon Wentworth.

'Well?' The King's question was levelled at the apothecary.

'He is easier.'

'Better?'

The man shifted uncomfortably. 'I

did not say that.'

'What ails him?'

'I can only hazard a guess, sir.'

'Well come, man. Let us hear it.'

The apothecary drew in his breath sharply. He looked uneasily first at the King then at Marian who was leaning tiredly against the tall back of Lady Grace's chair. 'It is my opinion that Sir Ralf is poisoned. I cannot be sure, but the illness bears all the signs. I have been many years in Pesaro in Italy. As you know,' he shrugged, 'it is a weapon used there more frequently than the poniard. Which poison — it is hard to say.'

Marian gave a little choking cry and came towards him with a rush. 'It isn't possible. How could it have happened? I tell you he ate and drank what we all did. We love him here, all of us.'

The King came to her side and drew her backwards to seat her in the carved chair.

'If you please, sire.'

The King raised his head from his

survey of the weeping girl to frown as Simon Wentworth spoke to him urgently.

'Quiet, lad. Your lady is distressed.'

'Aye, so she should be.'

Gloucester gripped the boy's arm and swung him round with an oath. 'Use more respect when you speak of your mistress.'

'Don't you see,' the boy panted, his eyes beseeching those of the King to mark him well, 'the cup was meant for you. It was from *your* cup he drank. You offered it to him yourself, sire, but it was from *her* hand you received it.'

10

Marian could hear voices round her as if from a grey fog, people arguing, some angry, others sharp with anxiety. She knew that unless she concentrated hard the blackness hovering near would engulf her, and it was imperative that it should not. Her hands gripped tightly down on the chair arm while she fought the swoon and at length half lifted her head. Simon Wentworth was still talking excitedly and she heard his words with dawning horror.

'But, Your Grace, My Lord of Gloucester drank from my cup and you, My Lord Hastings. Neither of you suffered any ill effects, yet the wine came from the same barrel. We drew all the jugs together. The servant gave one cup to Lady Marian and the other to me. *He* could not have poisoned the wine. I did not touch it. Yesterday she quarrelled with Sir Ralf over your visit. When Sir Ralf told her you were expected she was angry. I do not lie, sire. There were witnesses, Lady Grace and some man who was visiting. I have never seen him before. I think Sir Ralf said he had come as a messenger to Lady Marian from her father, Sir Humphrey Benford.'

'From Benford?' The King's tone had hardened. He swung round to Marian, still sitting in the chair where he had placed her. If her life had depended on it she could not have risen at that moment, though she knew etiquette demanded it. The King came to her, his habitual courtesy towards women making his tone solicitious.

'You are feeling better, Lady Marian? We feared you had swooned.'

She nodded, her eyes travelling to Simon Wentworth at the extreme end of the room. He appeared to have taken a defensive attitude, his back to the door, his feet planted solidly apart as if for greater reassurance. For once he had lost his usual sullen expression and was breathing noisily, excited by the determination to be believed. As her eyes caught his, he stared back accusingly, there was no attempt to evade her stare. He was convinced of her guilt. He believed her capable of this vile act. The suddenness of her awareness almost made her feel faint once more. She tried to conquer her rising panic and get up. At once the King waved her to be seated. Half turning she saw the tall apothecary behind her chair. He held a goblet of liquid and offered it to her.

'Drink, my lady. It will restore you. I went back to the sick room for the draught.'

Marian shook her head but the King insisted briskly. 'Do as the man says, mistress. It is wiser so.'

She drank the bitter draught obediently and the man took back the goblet. 'I must go to my husband . . . '

'No.' The King arrested her gently but firmly with a decisive gesture of his hand. 'You can do nothing for the

160

present. Master Carey, here, tells us he is sleeping. Besides . . . ' he paused, frowning slightly in his embarrassment at the delicacy of the situation, 'there are matters to be discussed.'

She met his gaze squarely, her lips parting soundlessly as she realised the implication of his last remark. Did he too consider her guilty?

'Master Carey, return to your patient. Summon us immediately if there is need, or if Sir Ralf's condition deteriorates in the slightest degree.'

The man bowed low. Only now he had become aware of the identity of the distinguished visitor to Compton. He gave Marian one final glance of cool professional interest, then withdrew silently.

'If you feel stronger, Lady Marian, there are questions we would like to ask you.'

'Of course.' Her answer was low but firm enough.

'You heard the apothecary. He seems certain now that your husband was indeed poisoned.'

'Yes, but how *is* Ralf?'

'There is no change at present.' The King was grave but authoritative. 'He is in less pain. Lady Grace remains with him. Lady Marian, can we return to the matter in hand? If this is indeed so, we must ascertain how and why the poison was placed in the cup.'

'It is impossible.' Marian could only repeat what had been her first reaction. 'I brought the wine from the cellar. It was our best, what we all had.'

'Your Grace,' Lord Hastings' smooth tones respectfully cut across her agitated reply. 'Will you allow me to take charge as your chamberlain? As sovereign and chief guest here it is difficult for you to press the matter as closely as an official could. Do you not think it is better handled officially?'

The King was about to protest. He looked from Gloucester's puzzled, distressed features to Lord Hastings' grave detached expression. He sighed and turned from the frightened girl and walked across the room to seat himself at the table some distance away.

'As you wish, Will,' he said quietly.

Lord Hastings crossed to stand immediately before Marian. Though courteous, his voice was coldly formal. 'You must realise, Lady Marian, that the poison in the cup was intended for His Grace the King, since you admit you carried the cup to him yourself.'

'Yes.' She looked up at him as fearlessly as she could. 'In common courtesy as hostess I carried the stirrup cup to the King.'

'Which he handed to your husband who drank from it and was poisoned — accidentally.' He paused before the final word. 'Let us be clear about that. There was no intention to harm Sir Ralf.'

'There was no poison in the cup. My God, do you think I would have allowed Ralf to drink it had I thought it contained venom?'

He did not reply to her question. He stood silent, his handsome face stern.

The events of the morning had sobered him and his brain was functioning with razor-sharp precision. The girl was close to hysteria, that was plain. The rising note in her voice told him that but he was bewildered. Had she indeed cared that her husband drank from the cup? She was looking distressed now, terrified, but that could be attributed to her fear of the consequences.

'Please tell us exactly in your own words what happened from the moment you rose to fetch the wine to the time that you knew Sir Ralf had been taken ill.'

'But I have told you . . . '

'Again, Lady Marian, and calmly please, if you can.'

'I went to the cellar with Simon. Oswald, one of the servants, drew from one of our best barrels. We drank from it at dinner last night. Simon carried one cup into the courtyard, I the other.'

'You came directly to the courtyard?'

'Yes.'

'You did not leave the wine unattended where a servant might have had opportunity to tamper with it?'

'No. Simon was with me. We came to the main door, then I sent him ahead.'

'Why did you do that?'

'Master Crosby came.'

'Master Crosby?'

Marian noted the rising cadence and hastened to explain. 'He is an impoverished gentleman who has recently acted as secretary for my father. He called several days ago to bring greetings and to ask if he could carry my message in return.'

'Simon Wentworth says he was here when Sir Ralf returned to Compton.'

'Yes. We had been riding.' She reddened at his cool gaze. 'We — we had William the groom with us. We had done so several times. Lady Grace approved.'

'I understand, Lady Marian. Your discretion in this matter is not in question. We are talking of the man

165

Crosby. He knew the King was expected here?'

'Ralf told me. He was there — but . . . ' she broke off and turned appealingly to the King. 'He had already told me some days earlier that the visit was likely. He had heard that the King intended to ride to Norfolk.'

'So you discussed the King with Master Crosby?'

'No — no I did not.'

'You discussed — other matters?' His tone was suave and she flushed again at the implication.

'We talked of my father. He brought me news of court.'

'So you *did* discuss court affairs.'

'No, that is — he told me the Earl of Warwick had left England. I was interested. Lady Anne Neville honoured me with her friendship.'

'That is true, Will.' Gloucester spoke from his position at Edward's side.

Marian warmed to his kindness in coming to her support.

'Crosby came at your invitation?'

Lord Hastings returned to his interrogation.

'No, no. I thought him on his way back to London. I had mislaid a letter for my father. He was delayed and he called to ask if I had discovered it. He was surprised and embarrassed to find the King at Compton.'

'You did not give him the letter?'

'Yes I did. I went back to my chamber to fetch it or rather another I had written.'

'Leaving the wine with Master Crosby or did you carry it with you?'

Now she understood his drift. Her eyes darkened with horror and a cold chill seemed to paralise every limb. She *had* left the wine with Crosby. 'Surely . . . '

Simon Wentworth answered for her. 'She sent me to the courtyard. I did not see what they did with the wine.'

'Well?' Lord Hastings waited.

'I put down the goblet and went to my chamber.' She answered him steadily but each word was forced out as if with a deliberate effort of will.

No one spoke.

'He had no cause,' she said at last. 'Why should he? I cannot believe . . . '

'Lady Marian, that is what must be proved.' Lord Hastings continued to watch her carefully and she was stung to anger.

'You think I knew — that we planned this . . . ' She found courage to rise so quickly that he gave ground before her and she ran to the King to lean over the table facing him, her eyes flashing with fury.

'Sire, he accuses me of plotting to murder you. Will you consider me capable of such a crime? I beg of you to hear me. My husband is gravely sick. I love him. Could I have stood by and tamely allowed him to drink wine I knew to be poisoned? He may die in there and I not with him.' She broke off with a choking sob. 'Please you must let me go . . . '

Ever gentle with women, the King was prepared to accept her plea but

Hastings was coldly practical.

'Sire, if what she says is true, she will be acquitted. We should need first to question this Crosby. At present it is unwise to allow her to remain free.'

'But I must go to Ralf. He needs me.'

'No, madam. His mother is with him.'

'Sire, I beg of you, on my knees if need be.'

The King rose, his face flushed with the need to appear unmoved. 'Lady Marian, we must deal cautiously in this matter. No harm shall come to you. You will remain under guard in this house while we seek to arrest this man. When he has been questioned we shall be more certain of the need to proceed further.'

'But why should I be judged guilty? If indeed he poisoned the wine, and I cannot believe it, why should I be implicated? I hardly know him. I tell you again and again, I love Ralf. He drank wine I offered him. If harm comes to him, do you think I can ever forgive myself?'

'Forgive me, Lady Marian, we have your word only that you love Sir Ralf.' The King was gentle but adamant. 'It may be that you had need to be rid of him. This plea cannot exonerate you.'

'They quarrelled.' Simon Wentworth edged forward. His voice spat venom. 'I heard them. Later that night in their chamber they discussed Crosby and the King.'

She turned on him like a tigress. 'Ralf had no suspicions regarding Master Crosby. If you heard aught then you heard that.'

'Aye, he believed that clearly enough but you spoke ill of the King and Sir Ralf said you held your father's views. Deny it not, mistress.'

A glitter hardened the King's blue eyes and his mouth tightened. He had no love for Sir Humphrey Benford. Were his suspicions of the man correct and was this girl tainted with her father's hate?

'We did quarrel over the King — for a while,' she was close to tears but she fought them back, 'but, sire, it was not as you think. We did not speak of the wars — it was on another count that we disagreed.'

His puzzled frown expressed doubt and he waited for an explanation. She was about to begin, then bit her lip in sudden shame. How could she speak of her fears regarding the King's visit? Even now it would cry her foolishness to the world and Ralf would be angered. Ralf — Oh God her heartfelt cry was for his recovery. How was he in that chamber where they would not allow her access? If he lived could he, too, believe this of her? The full horror of her position rocked her on her feet and she would have fallen had not Duke Richard of Gloucester hurried forward to support her.

The King's voice had grown increasingly cold throughout the questioning. He doubted her. God, it was true. Likely so, since a king went ever in fear of murderers. But that he should believe this of her, and Gloucester had not come to her defence.

Lord Hastings had gone to the door and called to someone outside. One of the King's men entered and, coming to her, touched her shoulder.

'Go with this man, Lady Marian,' Lord Hastings said quietly. 'You will be treated with the respect due to your standing. There is no formal charge against you yet, but it is the King's desire that you should be kept close until this matter is fully investigated.'

She turned to the two royal brothers and gave each one a mute and final appeal. Neither moved and she went at last out with her guard.

11

Marian was lodged in the second-floor room over the gatehouse. It had been furnished by Ralf as an extra guest room and was by no means the bare prison she might have expected. Though the new house contained no dungeons as the old keep had, Ralf had provided several guard rooms near to the guard captain's quarters on the ground floor. Lord Hastings sent extra cushions and warm coverings for the bed as the day had turned cooler towards evening. Supper was sent in, an excellent meal, but Marian sent back the tray untouched. She could neither rest nor eat. She paced the room from end to end her fingers shredding the fine kerchief in her hand.

No one came near her. Since Nan made no attempt to see her mistress, Marian thought that the girl had been kept busy assisting Lady Grace to nurse Ralf. There were no messages from her mother-in-law. Marian guessed that she had joined all others in judging her guilty. The guard captain, one of the King's own men, was cautious. Both he and Lord Hastings visited her briefly to ensure that she was comfortable before they retired for the night, leaving her in the charge of a young lieutenant on duty.

The hours had dragged interminably. She had questioned Lord Hastings about Ralf but he had little to tell her. Neither Lady Grace nor the apothecary had emerged from the sick room and he had heard no reports of any change in his condition. His kindness only deepened her agony of despair. If Ralf should die — and by her hand! She pictured him doubled up with pain, vomiting weakly, as she had seen him earlier, and there was no physician at hand. The apothecary seemed competent but how could she be sure? If only they would let her go to him. Had he asked for her, called for her in delirium?

She sank down at last in the chair, overcome with exhaustion of mind and body. It would be useless to climb into bed, though it had been made ready. She knew she would not sleep. She would remain fully dressed in case Ralf sent for her. She caught back a sob as she thought he might indeed die. Surely then the King would allow her close. Her head sank onto her folded arms laid on the table and she began to cry softly. It was the first time she had done so, despite all the fear and frustration of the last hours.

Her peril was great. She knew that. There could be no doubt in her mind that Giles Crosby had tried to kill the King. Obviously he had visited the house this morning with that very intention, knowing the King was in residence. He had used her shamelessly. Her cheeks burned as she remembered how completely had been her trust in him. He had seemed courteous and kind, those frank, open features inviting confidence. And he was a spy. Had she had sense and been less caught up in her own unhappiness at Ralf's desertion, she might have been more discerning. The man's very manner and appearance were tools of his trade.

A more terrible thought struck her. Men like Giles Crosby did not kill on their own behalf, but because commanded to do so by a superior. Her father had deliberately embroiled her in this plot, for undoubtedly she would be suspected as Crosby's accomplice. It might even be thought that the man was her lover. She shuddered at the thought. Lady Grace would be witness to the fact that they had spent much time alone together, had ridden out only with an elderly groom in attendance. There had been ample time to plot. Crosby had known the King's intention. He had been well prepared. How easy it had been. The poison might have been concealed in a ring or in the leathern purse he wore at his hip. If in a ring he would not even had need to get rid of her. It would not have been too difficult to come close and empty the poison into the cup she carried. Had he watched the party and judged when ready to depart that they would take refreshment, or had he planned to ride close to His Grace had there been need, to strike him with knife or dagger before any had been aware? Marian had made it so easy. She had left him alone with the wine — provided the weapon. How he would laugh with her father over the incident, but, her father? Had he left her to die?

Squarely she faced the thought. There seemed little chance of her acquittal. What chance had she to prove her innocence, make them see what a stupid, foolish dupe she had been in very truth? Perhaps they would torture her. It was not likely. Even such terrors could not take from her heart, at this moment, her fears for Ralf.

She jumped startled, as the door bolts were drawn and she rose, one hand on the table supporting her, as she turned towards her late visitor.

He came forward into the candleglow and she breathed her relief at sight of him. It was Richard of Gloucester.

'Do not be alarmed, Lady Marian. I come only to talk with you.'

'Ralf — he is not . . . '

'No, no. I have no news for you, I fear, but little comfort either. The apothecary reports he is in less pain again now and resting, but the risk is grave. I cannot hide that from you.'

'He has been worse?'

'Earlier there was a repeat of the vomiting. He had been fed with some broth. The result was not good and this has further weakened him. A herbal draught has been given him again. There is nothing we can do but wait and hope. Do not torture yourself with the thought that you could help him if only you were present. I assure you, it is not so.'

She looked up at him directly, challenging him to be honest with her. 'Do you judge me guilty, my lord?'

His grey eyes grew shadowed but he did not seek to evade her eyes. His hesitation was only momentary. 'We of our house learn from babyhood to trust few people. Even then we are frequently betrayed. I *want* to believe you. My heart tells me you are an innocent fly caught in a spider's web, but, I confess I must be cautious. Will you understand and forgive me?'

'Yes.' She nodded, turning from him with an exhausted sigh, and he came closer and seated himself near her, drawing her down to a chair at his side.

'You must pray, Lady Marian.'

'For Ralf's life? I have done it over and over again.'

'And for your own deliverance.'

'Lord, I begin to fear that even God has found me guilty already.'

'You cannot speak so. He alone knows what is in your heart.'

'And will give me my husband's life?'

He shook his head, his sensitive mouth warm with sympathy. 'I cannot pretend that experience has taught me to expect answers to my entreaties.'

'For Lady Anne?'

'Aye, and for my father and Rutland, my brother. Their tragedy was long ago. I was a child then, but I have not forgotten. I think I became fully grown from the moment I heard the news and more so when I heard George had forsaken us.'

'Yet you still trust to God?'

'Aye, madam.'

She was silent for a moment, then she said, 'Why did you come?'

'I could not leave you without news.' He stammered a little. 'I waited until the King retired. It seemed more politic.'

'I am grateful.' Her finger traced a circle on the oaken table. 'You spoke just now of a spider's web. Truly, my lord, a web woven for me by my own father. Is it not fitting?'

'You are bitter. It is natural. Again I tell you not to trust even in those of your own blood.'

He rose awkwardly. 'Try to sleep

now. I will send you news in the morning. It would be foolish to advise you not to fear, but I swear I will do everything I can to defend you from threats of torture. Ned is no monster. He likes not to see a woman in pain.'

'And My Lord Hastings?'

'Nor he. You are in safe keeping.'

'If Ralf is worse, they will let me go to him?' Her fingers caught at his in helpless pleading.

'I will do what I can. Let me go now. I will come to you again when it is wise to do so.'

She rose to curtsey but he shook his head, squeezing her fingers gently and withdrew. She heard him talking quietly to the guard outside for a moment, then the sound of his footsteps retreating along the corridor.

Now she felt strangely comforted. Gloucester had not said what she would have liked to hear, that he believed her word, but he had come. She crossed to the bed and stretched herself out fully dressed. Since there was nothing she could do but wait, it were best if she rested her body. If the need came to help Ralf in any way possible, she must not be exhausted.

She had been lying so perhaps an hour, when she heard again the sounds of her prison door being quietly unbolted. This time she was thoroughly alarmed and sat bolt upright at once. Gloucester had sworn to protect her from the torturers, yet had Hastings decided to question her more thoroughly before either of the royal brothers was awake? The house was not equipped for such work, but she knew well that many implements could be pressed into such a use, a riding crop, or heated iron. She found herself shivering from head to foot and had to force her trembling limbs to bring her upright.

The sight of her guard lieutenant did nothing to quieten her fears. He was alone and moving very stealthily. He made fast the door behind him then turned to her, cautioning her to silence with a gesture of his hand.

'What is it?' Her voice quavered, she was sure, but she tried not to break down utterly. 'Can a woman, prisoner or no, not be allowed privacy at this hour? Such conduct on Lord Hastings' part is unknightly, sir. Surely further ordeals can wait until the morning.'

'I do not come from Lord Hastings, lady,' the man said softly. 'You must trust me and not cry out. I am your father's man.'

As though expecting the sudden cry which she gave involuntarily, he shot forward noiselessly and covered her mouth almost brutally with his hand. 'Please, lady, you will betray us. True I am on guard alone, with two fellows of my own below, but the house is full of the King's men.'

'What are you doing here in the King's livery?' She whispered the words hoarsely as he withdrew his hand.

'We have been prepared for weeks for this purpose. When Crosby had done his work, to extricate you if possible.'

'And if not possible, to leave me to my fate.' Her tone was bitter. 'I see now my father loves me well.'

'Nay, lady, he made provision for you. I have arranged matters. You must come with us tonight.'

'From this house, with the King in residence?'

The man grinned. 'The King is well occupied as he always is at night and Lord Hastings similarly. Gloucester is shut up in his apartment. He is unlikely to walk abroad now.'

He reached to a chair where her cloak had been thrown when Lord Hastings had sent it up for her in case she had need of it during the chilly hours of the night. 'Come, lady, it is lucky your own cloak is at hand. You will need it out of doors. Let us not delay.'

She retreated until she was brought up sharply by the heavy bulk of the bed. 'Outside? You mean you will take me from the house tonight?'

'Surely, lady. If you stay here you will

die, either here or later in London. Will you burn alive for treason?'

'I cannot go while my husband lies so gravely ill.'

The man stared at her in blank astonishment and lowered the arms which held out the cloak ready to place it round her shoulders.

'You must leave Sir Ralf to his fate. Your only hope lies with us.'

She shook her head and he cursed under his breath at the stubbornness of women.

'Lady, I do not seek to frighten you with idle threats. The penalty for treason in a woman is death at the stake. If you stay you will be judged guilty and before that there may be the ordeal of the question.'

'I know it.' Her lips trembled and she turned from him to slip to her knees by the bed. 'God, do you think I have not thought of these things? To run is to admit guilt. I will not do that.'

The man bent down to whisper close in her ear.

'Think you Sir Ralf will aid you? He is powerless to do so, and doubtless after his suffering he will leave you to your fate.'

'No.' She covered her ears to shut out his insistent reasoning.

'Look at me, madam.' He forced her chin round and she stared into his hard, soldier's face. 'I cannot wait for you to have women's doubts at this time. I have my orders. You must come.' The final three words were grated out between clenched teeth. He was fast losing patience. 'The drawbridge is down to admit visitors from the village for the entertainment of the King's company. You take my meaning, I am sure. This I arranged. Such an opportunity cannot be repeated.'

She gave a sob of refusal, shaking her head from side to side while silent tears rained onto her clenched hands.

He drew in his breath abruptly and she was relieved to see him rise, but just as suddenly he reached out and pulled her upright with him and before she could even utter a startled cry his fist struck her sharply under the chin as he took her full weight onto his free arm. Blackness engulfed her instantly. Angrily the soldier pulled sharply at the cloak where he had flung it onto the chair again, wrapped it round the unconscious girl, almost stifling her in its heavy folds, against the possibility of her coming to and crying out. He lowered the shrouded form onto the bed for a moment and went back to the door. A second guard entered as he undid the inside bolt and beckoned the man forward.

'Is all clear?'

The second guard grunted briefly in answer to his superior's question.

'We must carry the Lady Marian. I was forced to render her unconscious. Hurry, man.'

He waited until the guard had left with his burden, looked hurriedly round the small room, then left.

Outside in the corridor he grinned mirthlessly at the guard on duty.

'Secure the bolts again. Wait two hours until we are clear, then leave this house.'

The man nodded acknowledgment as the lieutenant walked off into the unlighted corridor ahead.

12

A dull throbbing in her head and
feeling of deadly nausea brought
Marian to painful consciousness. She
moved only slightly and experienced
intensification of the pain above her
eyes. She could not tell where she was.
She lay in Stygian blackness.

The place was alien, she knew that.
Her nose told her that the stinks of
damp wood, pitch and cordage were
not to be found at Compton. She
forced her aching brain to think back.

The guard lieutenant had enticed her
to escape. She had refused since it was
unthinkable that she leave Ralf. He had
been angry with her. His face had
loomed close to hers, then she had
fainted. Obviously he had struck her.
She reached out a hand and felt her
face gingerly, whimpering as a bruise
on the left side of her chin was

identifiable as the result of the blow from his fist. But she had been unconscious for hours. Surely that blow had not been the cause.

Her brow wrinkled in the effort to concentrate despite the pain. She *had* come to and struggled, but her cloak had been wrapped closely round her body as tightly and effectively as any bonds. A man had held her close against his hard body as he rode. She had smelt the leathern harness he wore and his rank male sweat. His iron buckles and his breastplate had pressed cruelly against her body as he had firmly subdued her and he'd muttered harshly, either to her or his mount she could not tell.

At last the stifling heat of the cloak pressed against her mouth had brought back the faintness. She had fought it but the original blow had been ungentle and she had drifted off again. How far had they ridden from Compton and where was she now?

She reached out again in the

blackness to explore with her finger-tips. She was lying on a bed of sorts made of rough wooden planks. Her cloak had been placed beneath her. Attempts had been made to ensure a tolerable comfort and her mouth was now free of the restricting cloth. Obviously her rescuers no longer feared that any cries she made would betray them. The bed was swaying and she felt deadly sick again. The creaking of timbers above warned her of her sleeping place. She tried to rise, and struck her head against a wooden balk above her. The pain was severe and, added to the misery of her early suffering, was sufficient to reduce her to helpless, weak tears. She knew now that her father's wishes had been obeyed to the letter. She had escaped from Compton true to his orders. Only too well she realised that separation from Ralf might be final. She was aboard ship. The lieutenant had doubtless carried her to Lynn and she was even now travelling to France.

In the blackness, she sobbed out her despair and over and over prayed to God and the Virgin that Ralf might live and that he would not judge her too harshly.

A new noise pierced the blackness of her despair. This sound she knew well. Someone was descending the companionway. She kept silent and drew her body into a defensive attitude, her back to the hard wall of the cabin. The door was unfastened and immediately she was forced to shield her eyes from the sudden glare of a lantern as her visitor stepped inside.

'Lady Marian, I trust you are more comfortable now?'

She stiffened to the pleasant, easy tones of Giles Crosby's voice. 'Master Crosby,' she spat out the name in her utter contempt, 'I had heard that rats could not survive on ships.'

'Only sinking ships lose their rats, lady,' he replied unabashed, 'and I assure you that though this one is acutely uncomfortable and noisome, it is seaworthy enough. We shall reach Calais in safety.'

'That should be some comfort to you, Crosby. You are unlikely to find it in England.'

He hung the lantern on a bracket above their heads and she could now bear its uncertain light and was able to see the cabin more completely. As he had said it was cheerless enough and confined. The bunk, on which she had been placed, occupied all the space and the roof was low and rough hewn. The stench of bilge water rose to her nostrils from the opened door, but the air was fresher and the salt tang of it eased her sickness.

'Alas,' Crosby said with a faint shrug, 'I had but little success, but as you say, I am no longer welcome in England.' He had pushed the cabin door to and stood leaning his back against it, facing her.

'It would be foolish to plead that you return me to England, sir. Where do you take me?'

He smiled. 'I regret I cannot grant your request. We dock in Calais. Your father waits for you there. He followed the Earl of Warwick some weeks ago.'

'Then you bore no messages from him when you came to Compton. It was merely a ruse to get close to the King.'

'You wrong me. Certainly I came from Sir Humphrey. He *was* anxious about you and will be even more so now.'

'He will not be pleased to hear that you failed.'

He spread his hands wide, still smiling. 'Not entirely, I grant you, but if I have widowed you he may still reward me.'

Marian went white to the lips and his eyes gleamed in the lantern glow. His shaft had gone home.

'Are you truly for Lancaster, or anyone's hireling?' She recovered quickly, and returned to her wounding attack.

He bared his teeth, momentarily caught off balance by her contempt.

'Queen Margaret pays me, and I am her man. Can you say you are for York, mistress, or for Sir Ralf Compton?'

'I care not for factions, sir. I happen to love my husband. That is enough for me. I honour him enough to doubt that he would commit murder, whatever his sympathies.'

He had recovered his genial humour. 'Your opinions are outdated, mistress. If Lancaster is to survive it must take any means which offer themselves. Edward of York is a traitor to his King and a usurper. What matters it if he dies by the hand of an assassin rather than on the headsman's block?'

'First catch your lion, then skin him,' she flashed back at him. 'Edward reigns still in Westminster, and England supports him.'

'Let us not waste energy in reviling each other, mistress. I'm glad to see you so far recovered and will send you food, aye, and a change of clothing. You will wish to greet your father fittingly. I made provision for you before we set sail.'

She turned from him. She could not eat but she would welcome the means to refresh herself. He made no further comment and she breathed more freely when he left her to herself.

Her father was waiting on the quay. Apparently he had been informed of the ship's nearness to harbour and had come down to meet it. She was surprised. It was not usual for him to show any sign of affection nor yet anxiety. Perhaps, after all, it was concern to hear Crosby's news which brought him out in the wind and rain.

Despite her haughty withdrawal, Crosby himself assisted her from the boat, lifting her over the greasy stones of the harbour front and setting her down close to her father.

'You will not wish to spoil your finery, mistress,' he reminded her in his courteous, urbane tone.

Sir Humphrey hastened forward to draw her towards him and scan her face intently.

'God be praised. You are safe and unharmed.'

She faced him squarely, her eyes stormy.

'If I am, it is no thanks to you, my father.'

He ignored the remark and, holding her still, looked over her head to Crosby's smiling face, where he stood behind her.

The man shrugged. 'Edward of March lives still. I will make you a detailed report at our lodging.'

'Is my daughter in peril?'

'Aye. The plot failed but is known. Ralf Compton lies close to death of the poison I meant for the King.'

Benford's eyes narrowed. He stiffened then nodded. The quay was not the place to discuss their business. He indicated that he wished to escort his daughter to their lodging in the town.

Marian said no word as they walked the short distance, nor did she answer her father as he welcomed her to the house and bade an attentive serving woman show her to the room prepared. Icily she accompanied the woman above stairs, conscious that her father and Crosby had entered a smaller room at the rear of the house.

Obviously the room was cramped for space but comfortable enough. A fire burned in the grate and the bed looked inviting, turned back for her to rest. The linen was decidedly clean and sweet smelling and had been warmed ready for her. The serving wench hovered uncertainly by the door and Marian dismissed her curtly. She longed for the comfort of Nan's presence or even the disapproving but stolid security of Janet Thurston's. She crossed the room and flung the casement wide, letting in the cold air from the quay, heavy with the scent of stale fish, pitch, wood shavings from the boat yards, and the mingled smells of spices and wool from the cargoes of the various vessels in port. Her head ached abominably. At least the air was fresher, if not the fine pure air of the Norfolk marshes. She rested her cheek against the leaded panes and let tears rain down at last onto her hand clenched on the sill. Without attempting to try the door or to descend the stairs and leave the house, she knew herself to be a prisoner. Her father would have posted a man below to keep her close. In all events such an escape from the house would avail her nothing. Where in Calais could she go? She could not swim back to England to Ralf. Even now he might be dead or dying and in all events he would be utterly convinced of her guilt. Who would believe that the lieutenant had carried her from Compton by force?

When she heard the door open behind her she made no effort to turn. Her father's voice sounded oddly muffled as if he found himself unaccountably awkward in her presence.

'They have made you comfortable, Marian? This is a poor place.'

She refused to meet his gaze and continued to look out over the roofs to the sea, her hand clenching and unclenching in her distress.

He moved closer to her and as she still did not stir, he reached out and touched her on the shoulder. She drew out at arm's length as if some noxious creature had sought to defile her.

'Marian, lass,' he was concerned at her denial of him, 'you will let me explain.'

'Master Crosby explained it all. I have a father who is a liar, a murderer and a traitor.'

At last she swung round to him, her back against the wall.

His anger returned at her scorn. 'I'll not have that, girl. Traitor I am not. Henry of Lancaster is my rightful King. Sweet Jesus stands my witness, I do no ill when I seek to place him on his lawful throne.'

'Swear not by him who died to save your soul. You damn it to very hell. Tell me of your need to kill my husband. Explain that — do it well, father, for by Our Lady, I will swear to do my utmost to see you pay for that foul murder.'

'You know well enough Compton's death was accidental. Who could tell he would drink that which was offered to His Grace?'

'And had he drank it, Edward, the King, do you tell me you would then suffer no pangs of conscience?'

He shrugged, impatient now at the rising panic he sensed in her challenge. So far her anger held her from nervous collapse, but tears and hysteria were now close to the surface of her consciousness. Her scorn he could understand, her distress frightened him. He had no way to comfort her, nothing to say or do to alleviate her agony. He countered this incompetence of his own nature by summarily dismissing the cause of her pain.

'I am for Lancaster. All else is naught to me. Margaret is my Queen and yours. I shall take you to her. In time you will forget. When we return to England, the Queen will arrange for you a fitting match.'

'Then I'm to be married again.' Laughter and tears warred in her voice. 'In truth, father, I shall be the most married woman in England. Men will be chary of bedding with me, since they will be unlikely to see my gold, let alone live to use it.'

He brushed away her derision. 'We will talk further when you are rested. It is useless to wound each other. I'll send up the woman.'

'Father.' Her cry arrested him in the action of lifting the door latch. He turned.

'Let me go back. I cannot now be a pawn in the game. I served my purpose.'

'You talk foolishly, Marian. There is no retreat for you and well you know it. Compton is dead — or dying. By now you will have been judged. In England only the fire waits for you, while Edward reigns. Here in Calais we have some of your gold. More, I have ascertained, is banked in Burgundy. Hurst was no fool. He made provision for himself whatever occurred in England. In these times it was necessary. The

greater part of your fortune will be con-
fiscate to the crown. It is regrettable,
but when Henry wears that crown again,
and I am convinced it will not be now
long delayed, what is yours will be returned
to you and we shall not find Margaret
ungenerous.'

'And already you have chosen a mate
for me. Is it not so, father?'

'There are those I would honour.' His
eyes glinted as she leaned towards him
and spat deliberately. He stared at the
spot on the rushes where the spittle
glistened in the light from the fire. He
looked from it to the angry flush which
dyed his daughter's cheeks. Her words
carried clearly in the warmed air. 'Let
Crosby dare to touch me, I will kill him
and you. That is a promise, father.
Heed it well.'

His own eyes narrowed in the
recognisable animal, feral glint she had
seen before on that day when he'd told
her coldly to wed Ralf Compton. He
said no word, then, abruptly, he
dropped his gaze and left her.

Part II

13

Marian rose stiffly from her kneeling position, where she had been adjusting the velvet folds of the Queen's gown in a vain attempt to hide a panel from which a badly worn portion had been cut out by her dressmakers. Despite her efforts the skirt did not hang correctly but it would have to do. She crossed to the oaken chest where the mirror lay ready and carried it to Margaret. It was one of the few costly things the Queen still possessed. Presented to her by the young and elegant Suffolk when she had first come to England as a bride to Harry, so many years ago, she had been loth to part with it along with the rest of the gold and jewels she had managed to bring with her in her flight from England. She held the gilded thing up and the June light sparkled on the uncut emeralds round its edge, awakening them to a green, eerie glow. She made no comment on the gown's shortcomings, nodded brusquely and handed back the mirror after one quick scrutiny of her finery.

Her gown of scarlet velvet would do well. It added to her queenly dignity; more could not be expected of it since it had seen more than six seasons. Lady Catherine, another lady-in-waiting, handed her a single rope of pearls which she arranged to her satisfaction.

'So, ladies,' she said in that vaguely husky, accented voice which Marian had grown to half detest and half admire during the long months when she had served her as attendant, 'we will attend the King. It is unlikely that Louis will outshine us. His parsimony is well known. I have not found aught to contradict the notion since we came here.'

Marian drew back as the Queen, attended by her two elder women,

208

reached the door and Margaret summoned her to follow with an imperious gesture.

'Mistress Compton, we would have you accompany us. Our state is small, let us behave regally.'

Marian curtseyed, hiding her faint sigh. It was three days now since they had come to Louis's castle of Amboise near Tours, from Angers. Louis's Queen was heavy with child and the court had journeyed from the plague-tainted air of Paris, for the expected delivery. The King had feasted Margaret of Anjou and the remnant of her court with geniality, not untinged with condescension. It disturbed Marian to see the stately Margaret hard put to it to swallow the half-veiled contempt of many of his courtiers, and she *had* swallowed them with dignity. Even now she made a proud, regal figure, as she swept into the audience chamber on the arm of her son, Edward of Wales. No one could have guessed how she had dreaded this ordeal. Since this unpleasant interview could no longer be delayed, then she would carry it through with fortitude.

So Warwick had come and Margaret had agreed to meet him. For so long the rumours and gossip had enlivened court life. It was impossible. Margaret would not see the man. Never — never would she forgive the wrongs done to her cause. Yet, the Kingmaker was here in Paris and that sly spider, Louis, had appointed himself conciliator.

He stood up now to welcome the Queen and escort her to a seat on the throne-dais, then took his own place. The court hushed its murmurings as it bowed low at the Queen's entrance, and turned expectantly now to the same door from which she had entered.

Marian too looked at that door from her position behind the Queen's chair, then flushed as she saw her father enter, the ubiquitous Sir Giles Crosby in attendance. He was late. She had thought he had intended to absent himself, knowing as she did the intensity of his hatred for the expected visitor.

Yet Warwick too, in the end, had become naught but a Lancastrian tool. For weeks the Kingmaker had held Edward prisoner, forced him to sign death warrants for his favourites, to accede to the execution of the Queen's own father. Edward had become over-indulgent, easily taken unawares, and George of Clarence, his own brother, had deserted him and married Warwick's Isobel. For a time the sun had dimmed its splendour and Warwick seemed fair to 'unmake' the King he had made after Mortimer's Cross, but he had planned without Gloucester. The young Duke had gathered the King's supporters, ridden hard for Warwick's stronghold of the North and demanded that the Earl return to his allegiance and give up the person of the King. Since Edward had been willing to promise much, Warwick had given way. Edward was freed to ride back to London.

Marian recalled with a thrill what happiness that news had given her, where she had sat among Margaret's ladies in that grim fortress of Angers.

Crosby had brought the news, 'March reigns again in Westminster, though now as a puppet King. Warwick holds the power. Please God, he keeps it.' He'd glanced at Marian as he spoke and she had gone white to the lips. His nearness brought so acute a loathing, it was almost a pain to her to remain seated, without withdrawing from the Queen's presence or betraying her unease.

Margaret had shrugged disinterested. Warwick was as hated as his cousin, Edward of York. What mattered it which of them ruled England?

Crosby had later drawn close to Marian while the Queen talked with her father.

'I have special tidings for you, Mistress Compton.'

'Indeed *Sir* Giles,' she was wont to

212

over-emphasise his title of knighthood. Though unsuccessful in his attempt on Edward's life, Margaret had created him baron as reward for his services, and Marian never failed to remind him of her contempt for it.

He smiled at her apparent lack of interest. She interested him, this daughter of Benford, all fire and ice, so small, yet so determined in her hatred of him. He never allowed her the satisfaction of appearing to wound his calmness. He treated her with studied respect, his ease of manner, his joviality unabated by her disdain in company.

'You will thank me for them.'

'I doubt it, sir.' She bent her head close over her embroidery frame.

He watched her closely, his eyes twinkling. 'I shall be surprised if you remain unmoved when I whisper Sir Ralf Compton lives and rode with Gloucester to free the King.'

She gave one little cry and a dark spot of blood marred the white silk of the unfinished altar cloth.

Queen Margaret turned towards her, frowning at the interruption, and Marian lowered her head respectfully, her eyes bright with tears. Later, in the room she shared with the other women, she lay on her bed and made silent prayers of gratitude to God and the Virgin.

He lived. Ralf lived — naught else mattered now. They were separated by miles of alien land and water and more thoroughly by the barrier of judgment which had been laid between them, but he breathed, rode, worshipped, though she saw him not — and it was possible to feel again, love again, hope again, allow that hard cold shell which had wrapped itself tightly round her heart, to melt just a little in the knowledge that one day, God willing, she would be able to make him understand.

But despite Sir Giles Crosby's fervent prayer, Warwick had *not* kept the power. Once free, the easy-going Edward had thrown off his lassitude of the last years. He had tasted submission and found it not to his liking. He was Edward of England and no man's puppet. When Sir Robert Welles had risen against the King in March, Edward had taken the field boldly, swiftly dealt with the rebels and summarily beheaded the ringleaders. Warwick had fled to Calais.

Now three months later he was to greet the Queen in King Louis's presence.

The doors at the extreme end of the audience chamber were flung wide. Marian leaned forward as the great Earl was announced and he strode forward to come before the throne-dais. She had never looked on him before this. The Lady Anne she knew well, the Lady Isobel and their mother, the Countess, but Richard Neville was unknown to her.

He was shorter than she had imagined, though broadly built. He carried himself with more pride than Edward the King, and his features were fine cut. He was a Neville in truth with their fatal attraction for women. His brown hair showed the sign of recent anxiety. He had grey at the temples and there were distinctive streaks of white in the brown hair brushed sharply back from the high noble brow. As he bowed his head but slightly to the royal persons on the dais, Marian saw a faint frown darken that brow and his lips twisted in a hard bitter line. In a more conciliatory mood he would have resembled his cousin, young Gloucester, she thought. There was the same indefinable air of authority, of reserve, of stolid strength. It seemed inconceivable that he should be here begging for the favour of his erstwhile enemy.

It appeared that Queen Margaret thought so too. After one direct challenging glance at the man, she averted her eyes and turned to her son whose chair was but slightly behind hers and on her right side. He bent his fair head to listen to her.

Louis was speaking, welcoming My Lord Earl, his honeyed tones reminding the company of the happy occasion for which they had met, the reconciliation of two opposing parties. Warwick replied in one or two short conventional phrases of gratitude. He moved towards the Queen but she remained turned from him. Louis frowned. His fingers tapped in irritation on his throne arm, while he waited for Margaret to go part way to meet the pride of the Earl who had deliberately brought himself to seek her presence. His eyes sought those of Warwick and the Earl's met his half in proud disdain, half in bewilderment, then as the silence grew more menacing. Warwick stepped gracefully forward and fell onto his knees. A little strangled gasp went up from the company. The Queen turned back to him. Her dark eyes surveyed him coldly as he knelt before her.

'Well, My Lord Earl,' she said at last, her voice made harsher by emotion, 'I see you, after long years, where you belong, on your knees before your rightful sovereign and her heir.'

Again he made that very slight motion of his head, hardly to be described as a bow. Even thus, on his knees, he was a proud, unyielding statue.

'Madam,' he said, and there was no trace of emotion or faltering in the deep calm tone, 'liege lady, I come to offer my life in your service, to crave your pardon for wrongs done you and yours in the past, and to plead that I may be allowed to join my forces with yours to free England from a pleasure-loving and licentious tyrant. For this purpose I have come and it is my humble prayer that you will restore me once again to my true allegiance.'

Marian drew a sharp breath at the humility of the words uttered in so commanding a tone that no one in Louis's court could have doubted the innate nobility of the speaker. Submissive Warwick might appear to be, repentant he was not, and the Queen knew it, as they all did.

Her eyes flashed sudden fire and she leaned forward in her chair to peer closely into his stern, impassive countenance. For one dread moment Marian thought she would strike the Earl there before them all. King Louis moved again, restless in his seat. Perhaps he too thought the moment charged with tension. Warwick remained motionless, then the Queen sat back, waited some minutes then signalled her desire that he should rise, by a wave of one small white hand.

He rose and advanced as if to kiss that hand, yet still she held it from him, drawn tightly across her breast. Marian could see the tension in the white shining gloss of the stretched knuckles, then she extended it and he bent gracefully to give the kiss of a dutiful subject. It was done. The Kingmaker and the House of Lancaster were reunited. Now let Edward beware.

Marian's eyes caught those of her father. He held her gaze steadily. It was impossible to read his feelings. Other

Lancastrian nobles were standing silent, then as the high tension in the audience chamber was broken, they began to circulate again, to laugh and talk and edge closer to the great Earl. Warwick was not yet in favour, but his good will was now essential if they wished to remain near the person of the Queen. Marian sat thoughtful, her troubled expression following the imposing figure of the Earl as he drew close to the young prince.

Warwick was gorgeously apparelled. His black velvet short doublet was ornamented by a heavy chain of gold set with rubies. The hat slung over his shoulder bore a gold and ruby clasp worth a king's ransom. It was clear that he intended to impress. His bearing, his very manner said to Margaret, 'Ally yourself with me and the Lancastrian star will rise. Is it not obvious by your appearance that you cannot afford to ignore the solid worth of the Neville inheritance?'

The young prince's eyes followed the

splendour of the Earl's finery. A wry twist of his lips told Marian he envied the man his show. Edward was young, effeminate, his slim figure still that of a lad. Though charming and sensitive, his features lacked character. Marian could never see the boy without wondering how Margaret had come to bear him. During the weeks she had attended his mother, she had watched him closely. If this were the Lancastrian hope, he might yet reign in England. Certainly there were resemblances to Harry of Lancaster. The boy was moody and remote. He spent hours day-dreaming in his chamber or leaning over the battlements, staring over the country-side rather than perfecting the use of arms. Occasional flashes of temper proved him his mother's son, but he was rarely cruel. Marian found him, in fact, likeable and kindly but ill-suited to rule. He lacked the restless drive and streaks of ruthlessness she sensed in this man Warwick or, in young Glouc-ester and in Edward of York, despite his apparent indolence. Some had whispered that this whelp of Margaret's was not Harry's. Had Suffolk or Wiltshire been his sire? Marian would not have found it in her heart to blame Margaret if it had been so. The young, fiercely passionate, René of Anjou's daughter could not have been mated with a more unsuitable husband than poor saintly Harry. Yet the boy had the same love of religious ritual, the sincere admiration for beauty. More sensual than the imprisoned King, it was not unlikely that he was Harry's heir in truth.

Warwick excused himself and crossed to the door. Again the level of noise dropped in the chamber as if the throng was expectant, wary of some new ploy. When the Earl reentered he was leading a girl by the hand towards the Queen. Marian's lips parted soundlessly at sight of her.

Never had she seen the Lady Anne so regally garbed. Her white brocaded gown was edged with marten fur and, like her sire, she wore a fortune in pearls and rubies round her throat sewn subtly into the bodice of her gown and into the fashionable truncated hennin which held the delicate veil of finest silk which fell onto her bared white shoulders. She walked like one in a dream, looking neither to one side of her or the other. When her father drew her forward in front of the throne-dais, she curtseyed gracefully, her blue eyes lowered demurely, but Marian noticed that when she rose again at the Queen's gracious command, those eyes continued to look ahead, empty, as if she had deliberately separated her inmost being from the company in which she found herself.

Margaret regarded the girl with grudging admiration. Anne could not be described as a beauty but her features were delicate and regular. She bore herself with the dignity of a princess though without the flaunting pride which often accompanied such a poise. Edward of Lancaster had not failed to note the gentleness of her regard. He smiled and came forward to touch her hand in greeting.

Marian could hear no more of what was said, though she listened intently. Courtiers thronged round her and demanded her attention. It was ever so, she thought with a cynical *moue* of distaste. These landless Lancastrian gentlemen knew well her worth as an heiress, as those round Margaret knew Anne's. So Warwick had played his final move in the chequer-game of power. Anne was lovely enough, and of a nature to attract the sensitive young prince, and he flaunted her in all her wealth and splendour as heiress to half the Warwick gold and lands. Not for the first time, Marian felt an affinity with the noble girl who carried through the role her father had decreed for her with so serene an air.

Just once, as she reached the door on her father's arm, did her eyes betray a flicker of animation. She turned and saw Marian close to the Queen's side. For seconds the blue, almost violet eyes looked as if they would fill with tears, then she smiled at Marian, and withdrew at her father's insistence.

After the Queen had left the audience chamber, Marian seized her chance to escape to the peace of the inner courtyard. Tonight she was on duty in the Queen's chamber and there would be no time to brood or allow thoughts of Ralf and all that she had lost to sweep over her. The sight of the Lady Anne Neville brought to mind the days when Ralf had been courting her and also of Gloucester's views concerning him, which had so disturbed her at the time. Now neither of them had the man she loved.

As she hastened into the room she shared with three other ladies, Lady Mary sighed with relief.

'Mistress Marian, where have you been? The Queen has sent for you.'

'I am sorry, but I am early . . . '

'She is waiting in her chamber.'

Marian straightened her hair under the hennin and patted the folds of her skirt. Queen Margaret had a sharp tongue. It was not wise to anger her needlessly.

The Queen's adviser and friend de Brezé was closeted with her. Since she was reading a letter it seemed he might have brought news from England. It could not have been good for the Queen's brow was darkened and her fingers tapped an irritated tattoo on the table before her. Marian curtseyed low and waited for her orders.

'Mistress Compton,' Margaret turned to her at last. It was her practice to ignore kneeling or curtseying courtiers until it seemed they would faint with weariness. 'I have received a request from the household of the Earl of Warwick. You may know they left England in haste and the Lady Anne is ill attended. There are serving wenches, of course, but her ladies remained behind in England. She saw you in the audience chamber and expressed a desire for your company. I understand you know her personally.'

'Yes, Your Grace. The Lady Anne honoured me with her friendship when I was in attendance on Queen Elizabeth.'

Margaret of Anjou passed no comment nor did she allow Elizabeth Woodville's hated name to anger her. She nodded.

'You have no objections to leaving my household? Your father expressed none.'

'No, Your Grace. Since the Lady Anne needs me I would be happy to serve her if you will grant me leave to do so.'

'I must spare you. Warwick is our master.' She gave a harsh, barking laugh. 'Is it not so, de Brezé? Richard Neville orders the Lancastrian army since Louis has so decreed it.'

De Brezé bowed. 'Your Grace knows well it was my advice to you to accept this allegiance. It would be wise to humour the Kingmaker.'

He did not add the words 'at present' but they hovered in the air, as if spoken aloud.

The Queen smiled broadly and looked again at the letter in her hand.

'Aye. Well, Mistress Marian, get you hence. There is a messenger to escort you.'

Marian was glad to make her escape. Her heart was beating fast as she followed the Warwick retainer to the house set aside for his use adjoining the palace.

The place was in chaos. Servants dashed hither and thither unpacking furniture, clothing chests, plate and personal possessions. A serving wench emerged from an upstairs chamber and dashed downstairs carrying a basin covered with a blood-stained cloth. The girl looked frightened and Marian turned to her guide for information.

'Both the Countess and Lady Isobel are unwell,' he said curtly. 'The Lady Anne has her chamber here at this end of the corridor.'

A blowsy-looking child opened at his knock and Anne Neville rose from her seat near the bed. She had laid aside her hennin and taken off her jewels, otherwise she appeared as she had when her father had presented her to King Louis and Queen Margaret. She dismissed both the girl and her father's messenger and, as the door closed on them both, held out her arms to Marian with a little glad cry.

Marian held her close and both of them dissolved into tears, half of delight and half of distress.

'Oh, Marian, it is so good to see you, so good. I needed a friend in that awful room and then I saw you.'

'The Queen sent me to you, for a time at least.'

'The Saints be thanked. You will stay? You are not disturbed that I should ask for you?'

Marian drew away and looked into the tear-filled blue eyes. She shook her head mutely and Anne drew her to a seat near her own.

'My mother is unwell. I have just left her. Isobel lost her child, did you not know? Clarence is angry as a bear and my lord father says little but bites his under lip. It is a bad blow for them both but when will they think of Isobel's sorrow? She was like to die and it will be months before she recovers.'

'I'm sorry. How long ago was it?'

'Her pains began during our voyage. There was a terrible storm and then they would not allow us to land in Calais. Lord Wenlock had command of the port and he sent word that on the King's orders he must deny us.' Anne put up a hand to her brow as she remembered those terrifying hours in the stuffy cabin while Isobel screamed in her agony and her father raged in impatient fury on deck above their heads. 'Then they fired on us. Several cannon balls splashed into the water really close to our ship. We needed to get Isobel to shore to a doctor but it was no use. We lay anchored just outside the harbour for all the rest of the day and night before setting sail for Honfleur.'

Marian waited quietly for the rest of

the story but in the end there was little to say.

'She was delivered that night of a son. He died. That was last April.' Anne gave a twisted smile, conquering her tears. 'Perhaps God in His mercy saved that scrap from being a further pawn in our father's hands.'

Marian looked away, then Anne spoke again.

'Forgive me, Marian, I have not asked about you. I had heard — you have found peace in Queen Margaret's service?'

'There is no happiness or joy while I am kept from my husband, my lady. Tell me ought of Sir Ralf. I know he lives, nothing else.'

'You do not know you are a Countess? Edward created him Earl of Saxby on his return to London from the North. Ralf Compton rode with Richard of Gloucester to demand the King's release from my father.' Anne's voice trembled on that name and she lifted a nervous hand to twist a strand of fair hair which fell loosely onto her face, now that she had freed her hair from the confining bands of the hennin. 'My father feasted Richard and the other lords in the Great Hall. Sir Ralf looked pale, I thought, but as usual. I remembered that Duke Richard had not thought well of him and it appeared strange that Sir Ralf was so high in his favour.'

'Did Gloucester speak of me?' Marian's voice was eager.

Anne shook her head. 'We did not speak to each other,' she explained. 'The King has forbidden Gloucester's friendship with our family. Though the breach was healed temporarily from that time there was war between my father and Edward of York.'

'You knew I was accused of seeking to murder the King?'

'Yes, I was convinced this was a foul lie.'

'My father plotted the crime and I was to pay for it. No . . . ' Marian shook her head at Anne's shocked countenance, 'no, I wrong him. He intended to arrange my escape. I believe that truly, but had he failed, he would have left me to my fate.'

Anne Neville rose to her feet and crossed to her table where a crucifix and breviary had been placed ready.

'I have often wondered if I shall love my own babe, if I have one, or if I shall consider it a useful pawn like my father has found me and Isobel and apparently your father has found you, Marian. We talked of a child, Richard and I, one who would have my fairness and his strength. He's very strong, my Richard, though his looks belie it — and now . . . ' She broke off and Marian came to her and, taking her hands, kissed one of them gently. Anne's lips trembled but she went on. 'Now — now it seems that I shall never bear his name or his child.'

14

'You can go in, Lady Marian.' The Earl coldly stood aside for her as she rose from her curtsey. He had been closeted with Anne for about half an hour and she had been summarily dismissed from the room. Impatiently she had paced the corridor under the curiously watchful gaze of one of my lord's pages. Even with its length separating her from the door of the Lady Anne's chamber she knew it had been a stormy interview. Now the Earl had a steely glint in his grey eyes as he bowed in acknowledgment of her curtsey. She waited for a moment longer with her hand on the latch until he had descended the stairs, then she pushed the door open and entered.

Anne was crying quietly as she knelt at her *prie-dieu*. Her fingers clasped a small golden cross she sometimes wore round her neck but for the present she was too distressed to begin praying.

Marian dropped to her knees beside her and held her close while the tears rained down onto her clasped hands. They were both bereft of words and when Lady Anne at last conquered her tears, she bent and kissed Marian's comforting hand on her shoulder.

'I am myself again,' she said, as she rose to her feet. 'It was just that I couldn't help it. I knew it would come, of course, I've known it for days, since we came here, but while the words were not spoken aloud, I could push the thought aside.'

Marian rose too and waited while the younger woman seated herself on the bed.

'Your father has spoken of your betrothal?'

'Yes. Queen Margaret has given in at last. Her consent is obtained. I am to wed Edward of Lancaster within the month.'

Marian could find nothing to say.

Well enough she knew how inadequate words could be at such a time.

'I argued, pleaded. I had not thought I would find the courage, but somehow I had to try to make him understand. I am pledged to Dickon.'

'He was angry?'

'Not at first. He realised how difficult this would be for me. Since childhood Dickon and I have been close but circumstances have changed. I must put my duty to my family before private concerns. He looks high, my father. I shall be Princess of Wales and Queen of England.'

'What of the Prince? Is he willing? Did your father speak of him?'

Anne looked past Marian out of the window to where the battlemented towers of King Louis's castle could be seen close by. 'It seems he is most anxious to have me for his bride. Only Margaret has held out for so long. She is no fool. She knows well enough who will be the dominant power behind Edward's throne if he reigns in

England. My father is not named Kingmaker for naught.'

Marian hesitated then seated herself by Anne's side. 'Do you find him so unattractive?'

'Edward?' Anne turned quickly to scan her friend's face. 'No, he seems kind. There could be a worse match. Isobel . . . ' She broke off and Marian nodded in sympathy. Both felt a wealth of pity for Anne's older sister, wife to the blustering, drink-sodden Clarence.

Recent events had left George with no comfort but the wine cup. In their recent bid for power he had expected an easy victory. Had Dickon been with them . . . He had railed aloud against his brother's support of the King. They had a right to expect his loyalty. Had he not, with Clarence, been page and squire to their cousin, Warwick? Had he not learnt his skill at arms in the Earl's service? Surely Dickon's avowed love for Warwick's Anne would have held him to their cause. That alone should have sufficed without consideration of the contempt George knew well that Dickon held for the Woodville party.

But Gloucester had remained true to his motto. Loyalty bound him to Edward and it was Gloucester who had gathered the King's supporters and freed Edward. Now there was little hope of Warwick unseating his elder brother and placing George on the throne, and to crown his disappointment, Isobel, the whey-faced fool, had lost his child. No, George was in no humour to comfort his ailing wife and his fury had been further inflamed by Warwick's avowed intention of betrothing Anne to the Lancastrian heir.

Anne was his hope. If Isobel were not to wear the crown, Anne should do so. She was gentle and tractable. He could bend her to his will and with her her admiring husband for it was plain that Edward of Lancaster was besotted with Anne's pale beauty.

'God's teeth,' Clarence declared, 'has the world run mad?' First Dickon had been enthralled by her blue eyes and now this idiot of a prince who was good for naught but to make verses.

His soul had quailed, during his more sober moments, when he thought on Edward's vengeance if they should fail. Only occasionally had George glimpsed his brother in a passion but remembrance of it now turned his blood to ice in his veins. There had been times on that ship when he'd thought of throwing himself overboard, swimming to shore and placing himself at Wenlock's mercy and declaring himself repentant. But Warwick had been closer than Edward and George feared his father-in-law even more than his brother, at least while his nearness brought him within the Earl's means of repaying any treacherous move on his part.

So Isobel had wept in vain. There was no pity in George, rather a hard fist if she displeased him by her complaints. Fearful of husband and father alike the stricken girl had kept to her chamber and rarely ventured out. Anne could consider herself more fortunate indeed than her sister.

Marian rose and began to pace the floor. 'Lady Anne,' she said quietly, 'what we must remember is that Duke Richard may well believe that you are anxious for this marriage.'

Anne's eyes blazed with sudden fire. 'He knows that I love him,' she said simply.

'Then he may well aid you.'

'He cannot.' She dropped her eyes from Marian's direct ones. 'He will not. He is pledged to Edward. He will sacrifice me as my father will.'

'Can you be sure of that?'

'If he loved me he would come to me.'

'You ask a great deal.'

'If I could go to Richard, do you think for one moment that I would hesitate? I love my father and mother, Marian. Believe me I do, and I care for Isobel, especially now that she has need of me. If Richard were a beggar with but one suit to his back I would go

240

where he asked. Had he loved me so, he would have supported my father. God knows he had just cause. He loves not Elizabeth Woodville or her brood. Many times he has spoken of Edward's laxity, his easy morals. Had he stood firm with my father, he could have brought the King to his senses.'

Marian shook her head. 'I think you are wrong, my lady. Edward is not so easy to manipulate as one would suppose. Outwardly he is easy-going, amenable, underneath there is a hard streak and he has a good head for business. Edward's no one's fool. Duke Richard worships his brother, but he is just. If he remains with the King, it is because he believes the King's cause a righteous one.'

'Then there's nothing I can do but submit.' Anne looked anxiously at Marian who was for the moment lost in her own thoughts.

'My lady, you say you had no speech with the Duke of Gloucester when he stayed in your father's castle.'

'No, my father forbade it.'

'One of the things which most concerns me about my separation from Ralf is that he may think me guilty. He may well believe that I wed with him to aid my father in his plans, that I have no love for him. I have found no way in all this time to send him one message. Lady Anne, if you could get word to your Richard he would at least know your true heart, be in no doubt.'

'But how?' Anne's blue eyes widened in appeal.

'There is no way, no way at all? No one you could trust?'

Marian peered down at Anne's face, saw it darken with fear. She made a helpless little gesture with one hand. 'My father would kill me,' she said at last.

Marian shook her head decisively. 'No, by no means. You are too valuable for his plans.'

Anne got up and went to the window. Her fingers grasped the sill as if reaching for some comforting firm contact. Louis's palace loomed up at her from the moat which separated it from the Earl's lodging. Within its walls lay her future husband and the proud Queen whose cold anger terrified Anne. Marian waited. Once, in London, she had sensed in Anne a core of hidden strength. Just now she was frightened, bewildered. If that courage could be stirred, they might yet attempt to extricate themselves from the complicated web of power spun for them by their respective fathers.

Anne swung round at last. 'There is an archer in my father's company. When I was a child I lied to save him from some punishment. I forget what it was all about,' she shrugged. 'Perhaps I never understood, but he has always spoiled me.'

'He is here in the household?'

'Yes.'

'He would take the risk?'

'I think he would — for me if I begged him.' She closed her eyes momentarily. 'I pray the Virgin I bring

243

no harm to him, but what else can I do? Richard must help me. I can't marry Edward, I *must* not.'

'How can we contact him?'

'He taught me to ride. My father trusts him and has allowed me to ride out in his company. Since we came here I haven't sought to do so. I have had no wish to ride among these people who stare at me as if I were some freak at a fair, and my mother and Isobel have been ill and have needed me. Now Isobel is to go to Normandy with Clarence and I shall have more time. My father will not consider it strange if I request permission for both of us to ride with Wat Roper.'

'We must waste no time.'

'I know it.' Once Anne's mind was made up she was impatient to put the plan into operation. She reached out and touched Marian's hand in a consoling gesture.

'Write to your Ralf, Marian. Wat shall carry letters from both of us.'

The Earl passed no objection when

Lady Anne broached the subject of her ride the following morning. He glanced at her briefly and acquiesced with a nod of his head. He seemed thankful that she had accepted her lot and appeared to be in a much happier frame of mind. He dispatched a page to the stables to bid Wat Roper saddle the required mounts and gave his attention to some documents which had been brought in late the previous night and which he had not had opportunity to peruse. The Countess, as usual, had kept to her chamber and Isobel was distraught, anxious about preparations for the journey to Normandy with her husband. She chided the servants for their sloth, then almost in the same breath recalled them to begin some other task before the first one was completed. Marian could not determine whether Anne's sister was delighted to be accompanying Clarence at last to their own establishment or distressed at the thought of being now completely at that young man's mercy. On consideration,

Marian was inclined to believe the latter, but in all events the Lady Isobel was in no state of mind to be suspicious of her sister's intentions.

Relieved, the two conspirators hurried to their chambers to prepare for the ride. Marian had already penned her letter to Ralf. Indeed she had sat up most of the night over the task, writing and re-writing in a frenzy of anxiety that he should read through her words the love which was in her heart. The final draft did not satisfy her but since she could not better it, she joined the Lady Anne and handed it into her keeping.

Wat Roper was a taciturn veteran of many campaigns. He touched his forelock respectfully and with the surprising skill and courtliness of a noble lifted his mistress into the saddle, then performed the same service for Marian. He lacked height but was the typical English bowman, sturdily built with massive shoulders and a wiry body. His skin was weather-beaten under the rough conditions of sundry campaigns and his right cheek was puckered where a stray arrow had grazed and furrowed the skin but fortunately missed one of his shrewd, pale blue eyes.

They rode contentedly. The summer had not yet drenched the landscape with gold. It was warm but not unpleasantly so and the freedom from the constant surveillance in the Warwick household was remarkably exhilarating. They gave their horses their heads for the first half hour or so then allowed the pace to slacken and ambled drowsily along the French hard packed roads. Lady Anne exclaimed in delight when they reached the bank of a small stream and declared that she would dismount and refresh herself. Roper rode up immediately and obliged by assisting both women to dismount. He kept guard by the horses while Lady Anne and Marian sped down to the water, dipped in their kerchiefs and wiped their sweating brows, even allowing the icy drops to slide down their necks and into the low corsage of their gowns. When Lady Anne called for him to join them he complied after slipping the lead reins of the horses onto the branches of a conveniently placed bush.

He listened without comment when Lady Anne hurriedly and hesitatingly put forth her request. He ran a gnarled hand through his front hair, grizzled at brow and temples, looked at her long and carefully under his thick sandy eyebrows then held out his hand for the messages without a word.

Anne withheld them for only a moment. 'There is grave danger, Wat,' she said frowning. 'You will be careful, for yourself, not for us. You must save yourself if there is fear of your being caught. Destroy the letters. They are of little value to me beside the worth of your life.'

He smiled, and touched her hand in a half clumsy, half affectionate gesture then he tucked the parchments into the neck of his livery doublet.

'Aye, mistress. You can rely on me.'

'I love you well, old friend.'

He grinned again at her insistence then put out a hand indicating that no more needed to be said. She rose at once and they mounted and returned to Amboise.

The hot days passed with steady monotony in the Warwick household. Marian was not summoned to return to her duty serving Queen Margaret and she was grateful that she was allowed to remain in the Lady Anne's company. Isobel had departed with Clarence and the Countess now, somewhat recovered, spent more time in the Great Hall or with her daughter and Marian in the solar, embroidering and listening to a young page singing and accompanying himself on the lute. Louis's Queen was safely delivered of a son and the King rejoiced under the congratulations of the courtiers who thronged the castle. Edward of Lancaster became a constant visitor to the Earl's lodging, though the

Queen, after that first occasion, did not condescend to receive her son's promised bride. No mention was made of Wat Roper's disappearance and the two women began to believe that he was indeed successful.

In all this time Marian had seen little of her father. He was in constant attendance on Queen Margaret and she rarely left the side of the Lady Anne. In some respects their lack of communication was a relief to her. In his presence she found it difficult to hide the cold waves of revulsion which swept over her if he came close or tried to touch her. He had never shown himself an affectionate man, but his cold-blooded attitude to the attempt on King Edward's life, and his decision to abandon her if necessary, had given her absolute proof of his inability to feel love for her. Perhaps it was her own fault. She failed to understand his fanatical devotion to the Lancastrian cause. At all events now she was free of his surveillance and she was content that it should be so.

She was surprised when one morning some days after her ride with Wat Roper she was called down to the hall and found her father awaiting her. She greeted him civilly.

'Good morning, father. You have been busied of late. It seems some time since we met.'

He made no reply and she noted, with a sudden fierce stab of fear, that his mouth was held in a cold thin line, and his eyes glittered in the danger signal she had come to know and recognise. She moved towards him calmly.

'Is aught wrong at the palace? Has Queen Margaret summoned me?' There was a faint tremor in her voice. Had such been the case she would have been ill put to it to find an excuse for denying the Queen her services.

His mouth twisted sardonically and he reached into the leathern purse at his hip, and, still without speaking, held out a parchment in his right hand.

She hesitated and then at last he spoke.

'Do not be afraid to read the contents, Marian. There are no ill-tidings. The letter is in your own hand.'

At his insistence she had put out a hand to take the folded parchment, now she drew it back as though she feared the contents would sting her.

He came forward and, seizing her hand, folded her stiffened fingers round the letter. 'Your property, my dear,' he said softly. 'You will not wish it to fall into the hands of strangers.'

She stared down at her letter to Ralf, the letter which had cost her so many hours of painful concentration. The seal had been broken and the outer surface was darkened by one ominous blotch of brownish stain.

He paused in the doorway as he made to leave her, meeting her horrified gaze.

'The messenger met with an accident. Unfortunate, was it not? I am relieved that the contents were not urgent.'

She waited until the door closed after him then thrust the ill-fated letter into the neck of her gown, shuddering inwardly as the stained parchment crackled against her taut flesh. By the Saints they had done ill, she and Anne. Wat Roper had died for their folly. She must apprise the Lady Anne of the news, comfort her. Was not she, Marian, responsible for the death of a deeply loved servant? She had over persuaded Anne. Without her determination the attempt to contact Gloucester would never have been made.

By this time My Lord Earl would know what had occurred. She had said that Warwick would never harm his younger daughter, his most valuable possession at this move in the game, but had she been over confident? Anne must be warned — and at once.

She mounted the stairs in great haste, almost stumbling clumsily, her usual dignity forgotten under the sense of urgency which drove her forward. Her way was barred abruptly by my lord's squire.

'My regrets, Lady Marian, I have orders to admit no one to Lady Anne's apartments.'

I am her lady-in-waiting, as you well know. She has need of me.'

'Not at present, madam. Her father is with her. When he gives me leave, I will withdraw.'

Marian drew back. Her teeth bit down sharply onto her bottom lip and a thread of blood welled. She tasted the salt tang of it. She was afraid, not for herself now, but for the quiet, reserved girl, who had risked her father's fury to write to her lover. One glance at the man's set countenance told her it was useless to argue. She must await the outcome in patience.

'Will you inform me when I am allowed to wait on my lady?' She faced the grim-faced soldier with calm dignity. He inclined his head in a respectful salute and she withdrew to pace the length of her own small chamber in an agony of suspense.

Warwick would consider his daughter's conduct treasonous to his cause. Had the letter been intercepted by men in Queen Margaret's household? Had it indeed been read by Prince Edward? If such was the case, it might mean death to his hopes. What then would he do to the luckless Anne?

The Earl was irritated to desperation by the Queen's unyielding attitude. Isobel's child had died. His wife was ailing. He could no longer trust Clarence. It had been necessary to keep his son-in-law closely watched. Warwick knew well enough that the young Duke considered his own best advantage would be to return to his allegiance to Edward. Only the fear of Warwick's retribution if he failed, or Edward's justifiable rage if he were caught and brought before his elder brother for judgment, kept him in France still allied to Warwick and Queen Margaret.

To add further fuel to the Earl's

wrath, his moon-calf of a daughter had committed to parchment the feelings she had for her cousin, Gloucester. No, the Earl must be livid with temper.

Tired out by her restless pacing, Marian at last sank down onto a stool and reached for her embroidery. She must find something to do, since she could not go to Anne to discover the extent of the Earl's knowledge. As no one came with a message, and the light failed, she was forced in the end to sit on in the darkening chamber unable to continue with the task. She should have felt hungry since it was now past the time for dinner, but she could not force herself to descend to the hall to eat with the members of the Warwick household.

When the Earl's squire came to her door at last, she was almost startled. She had sat alone for so long and had expected to do so throughout the night.

'My Lord Earl requests that you attend the Lady Anne in her chamber. She is ready to retire.' The man's voice was respectful but he peered at her, then curiously past her into the darkness of the room behind. She had not felt the need to rise and kindle the rushlight and she saw he was puzzled that she had stayed so during the evening hours.

She thanked him, waited until he descended to the hall and sped to Anne's room, jerking her mistress's door open in her haste. The room, like her own, was in darkness. As her eyes grew accustomed to the position of the furniture she saw that Anne was resting on her bed, her head turned away from the door. At first Marian believed that she had fallen asleep, then she glimpsed the crumpled state of her mistress's gown and the light from the window glimmered on Anne's fingers gripping tightly to the edge of the sheet, then relaxing and moving again convulsively. Marian gave a sudden exclamation of pity and hurried to her side.

'My lady, do not distress yourself. Let me help you. First I will light the candles.'

Anne made no answer and Marian quickly lit the candle in its holder near the bed and looked down at her friend.

Anne had been weeping, but it was over now. She lay sprawled against the silken cover, her lips tightly held in, her great eyes wide with sorrow and pain.

'Your father knows?' Marian knew the answer but she pressed on. 'Did he read your letter?'

There was a flicker of Anne's eyelashes. 'Wat is dead,' she said at last in a whisper.

'Yes, I know. I am sorry — but, Anne, it was quick. He must have been attacked and died in the struggle. He was a soldier. He would have wished it to be like that.'

'He need not have died.'

'Anne, you cannot blame yourself. How could you have foreseen this? You have been spied upon.'

'We should have realised that my father trusts no one.'

To this there was no adequate reply and Marian seated herself on the bed and reached out for Anne's cold little hand.

'What did he say? Did anyone of the Queen's household read the letter? Do you know?'

'No, the letters were brought directly to him. He paid the spy handsomely. So he informed me. Prince Edward is ignorant of the fact that I have no regard for him and long only for Dickon.'

'Praise the Saints. Matters might be worse.'

'This has determined my father to hasten with the betrothal. He has gone to Queen Margaret to demand that we leave for Angers immediately.' There was no tremor in Anne's voice. She appeared as calm as if she were by her parents' side in the great hall of Middleham receiving dignitaries.

Marian knew well that the girl was deeply shocked by Wat Roper's death. It was useless to offer comfort tonight. She rose and touched Anne's shoulder. 'Let me help you undress. You will feel better after you have slept.'

The girl winced sharply and drew back, gritting her teeth to cover a louder cry of pain. Marian stared at her, wide-eyed.

'You are hurt. Did your father strike you, lady?'

Anne rose quietly and beckoned her to assist her with the fastenings of her gown. Marian complied, her fingers suddenly gentle. As the Lady Anne's shift was revealed Marian checked at the sight of slight blood-stains. When the shift was finally discarded, Anne turned towards the candlelight and Marian cried out in horror at the great welts left by the Earl's brutal use of a belt or riding whip. Anne said no word but turned from her, and, slipping into bed, drew up the linen sheets to hide the marks of her shame.

Marian went to the door and summoned a page. There were always several waiting to carry messages or dicing at the head of the stairs.

'Bring warm scented water to My Lady Anne's chamber,' she said sharply.

'Hurry now.' She herself went back into her own room and, lighting a rushlight, held it high to search among her possessions in the small chest which had been carried to the Earl's lodgings from the room she had shared with the Queen's ladies. When she returned to Anne's bedside, the page had already brought up a heavy pitcher and clean napkin which he had placed ready to hand on the wooden chest near the window.

'Sit up, my lady,' Marian said firmly, 'your hurts need attention.'

Anne drew the sheet high up round her shoulders. 'Leave me, Marian, please.'

'My lady, I know what to do. Tomorrow you will be so stiff it will be well-nigh impossible to walk, let alone ride. Believe me, I am not without experience in these matters.' She smiled wryly at the other girl's stricken face. 'This salve will work wonders. My old nurse has used it on me, often.'

At her gentle insistence Anne sat up and threw back the coverings. Marian bathed the weals in warm water, gently touched them with the napkin and, barely touching the bruised back, soothed in the healing ointment.

'There, isn't that better?' She eased Anne back on the pillows, pushing back the waves of soft fair hair which had fallen onto her mistress's face.

Then and only then did Anne allow herself to cry but there were no anguished sobs, only the gentle tears which would ease her breaking heart. Marian said no word as the warm moist drops fell onto her hand. She drew up the covers and moved to extinguish the candle.

'Rest now. Try to sleep. I promise, things never appear so terrible in the morning light.'

At the door she paused. 'Was it one of your father's men who followed Wat? Did he tell you?'

'No.' Anne's whisper reached her across the now darkened room. 'It was a creature of your father's, one Giles Crosby.'

15

Marian's healing salve did appear to work wonders, for, much to the Earl's relief, Anne was found fit enough to ride the following day. In his blustering fury of the day before he had marked the girl. Now he half-regretted the impulse. His hasty discussion with his old crony, Louis, had resulted in the wily King's insistence that Queen Margaret should agree to the betrothal of her son with Warwick's Anne immediately and they had both found an ally in the younger prince. Edward was willing and eager to possess Anne as his promised bride and to have the contract duly ratified by Holy Church. Reluctantly Margaret agreed to her party leaving by first light for her castle of Angers.

Anne rode quietly behind her father, with the anxious Marian at her side, ready at once to call for a litter for her lady's use if necessary. Edward had ridden over at the commencenent of the journey to speak with his betrothed, his young face flushed with excitement and pleasure. Under her father's watchful eye, Anne greeted him civilly but with reserve. Warwick breathed more freely when the Queen sent a curt command to her son to ride alongside her, and the boy bowed to the two younger ladies and withdrew from their side. The Countess of Warwick travelled in the carriage with her older waiting women and some of the baggage. Indeed there would have been little room for Anne had she decided that she was too stiff to ride.

Soon after the beginning of the journey Marian's temper was sorely tried by the presence of Sir Giles Crosby. He rode up, doffing his hat in a low bow to them both, with apologies for Lady Marian from her father.

'Sir Humphrey regrets he is unable to accompany you, Lady Compton,' he said in his agreeable manner. 'He is detained in Amboise for some two or three days on the Queen's business. He hopes to arrive in Angers in time for the solemn betrothal and meanwhile has requested that I make myself responsible for your comfort and safety.'

Marian shot a swift glance at the Lady Anne. She seemed unaware that this gallant stranger was the man responsible for Wat Roper's untimely death, and the savage beating she had received from her father. She inclined her head in answer and, unwilling to acquaint her mistress of the man's duplicity and further distress her during the ride, Marian was forced to swallow her mounting rage and keep silent. She contented herself with murmuring, 'I am sure your solicitude is unnecessary, sir, since My Lord Earl of Warwick has assured me of his protection while I serve the Lady Anne here.'

Crosby bowed, his white teeth flashing in a smile. 'Care of you has ever been a sweet trouble to me, my lady.'

Marian tossed her head and urged her mount forward, her fingers tightening in anger on the reins. Despite her cool reception of him he remained by her side during most of the morning and was not far distant later, after they had halted for refreshment.

Anne had come to accept her fate with a kind of dulled detachment. She smiled at Marian's fears for her health and seemed cheerful enough, but Marian guessed her thoughts were miles away in London where Richard of Gloucester was busy about his brother's concerns. Marian's own thoughts winged after them. Was Ralf too about the King's business, My Lord Earl now in truth?

Angers proved a formidable fortress. Both women gave a shudder as they approached the huge grey mass of rock and even the Countess was heard to comment that the place seemed inhospitable. The Queen's arrival threw the place into a hive of activity and Marian was thankful to find Giles Crosby had little time to pester her with unwanted attentions.

She was to remember all her life the solemn pageantry in the Cathedral that made Anne Neville the betrothed of Edward of Lancaster. Queen Margaret had been forced to the match and she summoned up the final reserves of wealth to do honour to the occasion. Castle and church were bright with the jewelled colours of brocades and rich velvets. Young Edward was resplendant in white silk, embroidered with the red rose of Lancaster and the swan of his own personal cognizance.

Anne appeared pale and controlled in a gown of palest blue, a collar of sapphires encircling her slender throat and the crystals and pearls, with which her gown was encrusted, reflecting with glimmer and dull sheen the light of hundreds of candles lit in the Great Hall as the company feasted the royal pair later that night. Marian noted that she ate little but turned with a wistful smile and a courteous attention to her young bridegroom's whispered pleasantries. Though the young couple were not yet to be bedded, since the Queen had refused to allow consummation of the marriage until England was Lancastrian again, Marian knew that Anne's smiles were forced. These holy vows bound her to Edward with an indissoluble tie. Though not yet a bride, she must consider herself Edward's Princess of Wales and she must put all thoughts of Dickon from her heart from this day forward.

The Earl had agreed grudgingly to the Queen's conditions. Anne would be Princess of Wales and she was to stay in the household of the Queen at Angers until their business in England was concluded. He had already decided that action was now imperative. If the faltering Clarence were to swerve in his allegiance, then much of their striking force would be lost. He determined to sail soon for England and challenge Edward for power. By the end of the month he had left Anne in the Queen's charge and soon he and Clarence would sight their own land again.

Marian fretted against the confinement of the fortress. Now, once more, she was under the watchful eye of her father and, though she remained Anne's principal attendant and confidante, she found the Queen's hauteur, increased by hostility towards her new daughter-in-law, extremely hard to bear. For Anne's sake she was determined to bear up and both women knew their chances of sending more messages to England were at an end. From time to time Marian would look up from some household task or from crossing the courtyard to find Sir Giles Crosby watching her sardonically and she gave a shudder of fear when she thought how easily he held her in his power.

August days passed into September and the court waited eagerly for news of My Lord Earl. Margaret was constrained to join King Louis in Paris again. Only Edward seemed to care little. Marian found the change in his personality bewildering. Previously he had seemed half dreamer, half arrogant boaster, always dominated by his mother, now he seemed suddenly more mature, yet still the Queen's influence held him from his bride and, if he chafed at the delay in his possession of her, he gave no sign. At all events Anne made no secret of her relief that matters should continue so. Marian mused on the coincidence which made Anne a virgin bride still, as she herself had been until her marriage with Ralf.

She was to recall in later years how it seemed that it was ever Crosby who brought her ill news.

Seated in the pleasurance with the Queen and Anne she was surprised when he was announced by a page. He had been missing from the palace during these last days.

'My Queen, Warwick has landed and all is well. From all parts of England men have risen to support him. Edward fled to the North to summon aid and at

Doncaster Montecute roused the city against him. He, with Gloucester and the other Yorkist lords, took ship for Holland.'

Margaret's face flushed with the joy of victory.

'And the King my husband?'

'My Lord Earl fetched him from his prison in the Tower, arrayed him in royal robes, since it is said he had been ill-attended and ill provided for. He is even now in Westminster Hall and reigns in state.' Crosby laughed joyously. 'Queen Elizabeth, the usurper's wife, is mewed up in Sanctuary. She is near her time. If she bears Edward yet another daughter it will be in straitened circumstances.'

'God is good.' Margaret rose and gestured hurriedly to her women. 'Ladies, attend me in my chamber. We must write to My Lord Earl and congratulate him and to our husbands. At last we may consider what is next to be done.'

'Why, madam,' Crosby grinned impishly, 'we must pack our bags and join our good King Harry in England. He must have longed so many years for his true wife to comfort him.'

The Queen turned and looked at him sharply but there seemed no guile in his manner.

' 'Tis yet early days for us to venture ourselves in England,' she reminded him. 'We will first consult with King Louis.'

Crosby lingered in the small garden while Anne continued nervously with her embroidery and Marian challenged him with her eyes. The prince was not present.

'I know not whether Sir Ralf Compton accompanied the King,' he said meaningly. 'If not he might find life difficult in England at present.'

'If My Lord Earl,' Marian stressed Ralf's new title deliberately, 'could do so, doubtless he attended King Edward.'

'Um.' Crosby smiled at the Lady Anne. ' 'Tis rumoured that Duke Richard has got himself a son — a bastard it is true, the child of some serving woman in the service of the Duchess of York. A pity the Lady Elizabeth Woodville is not more accommodating, still so many daughters.'

Marian rose and folded the altar-cloth on which she was working. She knew well enough, and so did Crosby, he had dealt Anne a blow to the heart. Had he not seen her letter to Duke Richard?

'Lady Anne, the Autumn day grows chill and foul humours rise from the city,' she said crisply. 'Let us go in.'

Anne flashed her a glance of gratitude and they left Crosby alone with his triumph.

Crosby's poisonous words had truly found their mark. Once in the shelter of her own chamber Anne broke down and wept bitterly. Holding the stricken girl close in her arms, Marian could not but feel heartened. Until this moment Anne had accepted her fate too easily. It were as if some barrier had been erected between the girl herself and

273

reality. Now she had been forced to face the facts in their stark ugliness. During the weeks which followed Marian was pleased to see Anne come to life once more. No longer did she allow Margaret to openly shame her before the court. On each occasion she rose with silent dignity, and, without requesting permission, left the Queen's side. Margaret began to recognise in Warwick's younger daughter a woman worthy of her mettle, and, though she could not like the girl, treated her with grudging respect.

Autumn had now passed into the early days of Winter. Marian had expected that by now they would have been once more in England, yet the Queen lingered. Louis procrastinated and the Queen was chary of risking her darling's life in open conflict. True Edward of March was now living on his sister Margaret's charity in Burgundy, hoping against hope that his brother-in-law would support him in a last desperate challenge to Warwick, but he might yet return to England. No, she would wait awhile until Warwick was yet more firmly in control, England completely his. Her mouth closed in a tight line when she received news that Elizabeth Woodville had at last produced an heir in Sanctuary. So March had a young cub, a rival to her own Edward and named like him. Well might March fight yet more fiercely to protect his own heir. The time was still not ripe, so the Lancastrian party tarried in France while Warwick cursed at the delay.

Though the day was chill Marian led Anne one afternoon to the secluded pleasurance where Crosby had revealed the tidings of the King's defeat. Here, at least, for a short time the two women were out of sight of the Queen and her elderly watchdogs. Anne's teeth chattered but she gathered up her velvet skirts and ran down the pathway swept clear of snow and slush.

'Oh, Marian, the air is like wine.

Come and race me. Let us walk near the arbour.'

Marian stumbled on some hidden slide and fell. Anne turned, conscience stricken, and ran back to her companion but an archer who'd been standing by the tower hastened to the rescue.

He reached down to help Marian to her feet. When she laughed up at him, denying the need for his assistance, he bent down and whispered urgently in her ear.

'Stay there for one second, my lady. Let me help you. Lean on my arm. I have been waiting all day for a chance to speak with you.'

Marian stared at him, now thoroughly alarmed, but his face was unknown to her and his expression was all innocent solicitude.

'There is a seat in the arbour, lady. Let me help you there. Dissemble, please. Make more show of an injury.' His tone was insistent and she limped at his side while Anne walked anxiously by her side. The man smiled encouragingly.

'Trust me, Lady Compton. We could not have a better opportunity to speak privately together. There is none by. If the Lady Anne will keep watch and send any servant who approaches for aid, this accident will well serve our purpose.'

Anne nodded briefly. Instinct told her to trust the man and in all events, how could he harm them here so near the palace?

The pleached arbour formed a shade in summer. Now it was deserted, offering only slight shelter from the wind. As Marian leaned on her helper's arm she saw a man move within its shadow and stand limned against the starkness of its branches. She did not need for him to put back his hood to know him. She gave a little sob, half appeal, half delight, and was enfolded in two roughly clad arms and held tight against his leathern jerkin.

'Marian, my wife, I had not thought

to have you close.'

Anne turned hurriedly to the archer. 'Go back with me to the pleasurance, man. We will walk and talk together. If we are seen we must immediately feign concern for Lady Marian and send for help as you said. Marian, be swift. The Saints know I understand how you feel but if Ralf is discovered here . . . ' She broke off and Marian nodded and withdrew from the circle of her husband's arms. 'A few minutes only, lady. I will be brief — for all our sakes.'

'Then I will keep watch as you have done for me and Dickon.'

Ralf drew her into the arbour and laughed at her concern. 'Fear not, love. I have been in Paris some time waiting my opportunity to get a message to you. God's teeth you are well mewed up, like a nun in a cloister.'

'You come from Burgundy?'

'Aye, love.'

'The King?'

'Is well.' He grinned. 'He might have sent his regards had I thought to inform him of my journey. He is over-busied with preparations for departure.'

She drew a breath of cold pure air. 'He is ready for England?'

'Soon, my love, soon. Burgundy has been constrained to give aid. England will soon be Yorkist again.'

'Ralf, you are recovered, truly?'

He bent and nuzzled her ear, laughing at her distress. 'I would I could convince you how much I am recovered.'

'You do not think — believe that I . . . '

'Love, do you think me a crass fool?'

'Oh, Ralf.' Weak with relief she clung to him. It was impossible to comprehend the wonder of it. Here he was, solid, reassuring, tantalising as ever, within her reach. She could touch him, feel the roughness of his unshaven cheek and know he trusted in her love. Tears rained in a flood onto the hand which held her own in a tight clasp.

'I tried to write. Our messenger was taken. Giles Crosby revealed the truth of it to my father and the Earl.'

He frowned at Crosby's name. 'The man is endowed with the devil's luck.'

'Ralf, what do you here?'

'I came to see you were safe.'

'Then you still trust me?'

He grinned. 'It was not difficult to gain entrance. The palace teems with strangers. Perkin, over there, is in our pay. Never mind how I know that — I do. I have been trying to contact him for two days. I dared not approach you openly. He was to bring you my messages.' He thrust a sturdy package into her hand. 'My mother's letter to you is within, as mine is. I had not thought to have actual speech with you. You are not truly hurt?'

'No — the archer persuaded me to make the pretence.'

'God be praised.'

She checked as the sound of high-pitched laughter sounded from the garden. Two of the French Queen's maids sped round the corner of the curtain wall, pursued by some youthful squire. Ralf drew Marian close against the wooden supports of the arbour.

One of the girls squealed as her captor swooped. Marian heard the Lady Anne join in the general mirth. A flood of hasty French followed and the party moved off. The squire's voice was raised in mock anger, but it was clear they were all three preparing to re-enter the palace. Marian breathed again.

'Ralf, you must leave.'

'I will, never fear.'

'That you must, My Lord Earl.' The Lady Anne paused as she came to the arbour entrance. 'Those three may not be the only people in the palace seeking fresh air. It would be madness to linger.'

Ralf pulled Marian gently away from him and bent to humbly kiss her hand.

'Duke Richard will be overjoyed that I have seen you and can carry comforting tidings of your health, lady. He feared for you.'

She coloured and lowered her head. 'He knows — understands?'

'He suffers.'

She raised her head, blue eyes challenging. 'Not entirely, or was I wrongly informed?'

Ralf's eyebrows swept up comically. 'You mean Alys's child?'

'Is that her name?'

'Duke Richard is no saint, lady.' Ralf eyed her, his lips curling wryly. 'Were you to believe that you would be fool indeed.'

'She loves him — Alys?'

He shrugged. 'I know not. You have been long denied him.'

'He chose that it should be so.'

'Nay, lady, you know well the situation cannot be mended. Have courage.'

'For what, my lord? I am Edward of Lancaster's bride.'

He made a gesture of dissent, but could not avoid her clear gaze. 'There are means, my lady. The Pope could be asked to grant annulment. I know Gloucester has not, even now, given up hope. He loves you well.'

Her lip trembled. 'Tell him — tell him my heart is not changed — but that he is not to distress himself. Edward is considerate.'

He squeezed her hand, kissing the palm once more. 'I must go. As you say, I would find it impossible to extricate myself from this coil if I am found here. God keep you both.'

For one breathless second he held Marian close once more.

'Ralf, take me with you.'

'Love, it is impossible.'

'But . . . '

'Burgundy is no place for you. You are no camp follower. Even should I be able to take you from Paris, I cannot keep you safe. The Lady Anne needs you still. Wait for me, love. When the King has his own again, nothing shall keep you from me.'

She let him go, though she was choked with silent tears. Anne stayed by her till she mastered herself. When they left the arbour, Perkin the archer was nowhere in sight.

It was impossible to say how she was able to control her words and actions during the following hours. When the two women re-entered the palace they were called to Queen Margaret's chamber so Marian was unable to so much as glance at the package Ralf had given her. She felt its hard bulk pressed close against the softness of her breast where she had thrust it out of sight into the bosom of her gown. There it appeared to give out waves of comforting warmth, a fire which threatened to cry aloud its presence, so scorching was it, towards evening when Marian's whole soul demanded that she be allowed to withdraw to the privacy of her own room and read what he had written. There had been so little time. There had been questions, thousands of them, she had longed to ask of him, but her need to have him away from the palace had thrust away all thirst for knowledge. A thrill of pleasure swept through her when she thought Lady Compton still had belief in her. She had thought her mother-in-law her bitter enemy, but Ralf had said she had written her love for her daughter. Marian flushed as she found the Queen's sharp eyes dwelling overlong on her. Had she been indiscreet, unwatchful? Had she allowed herself to escape into rosy dreams when Queen Margaret had made demands on her, but the Queen turned back to Lady Anne, so apparently she had not spoken to Marian. She was merely curious with the woman's instinctive suspicion of another's happiness. Marian gave her attention to her embroidery. She must not allow thoughts of Ralf to rise unbidden and make her face flush with rosy colour or her heart beat more quickly, and the ache in her body grow yet more intolerable.

The young Prince Edward lolled moodily on a chest near the window, his insensitive fingers plucking discordant notes from his beribboned lute. The Queen looked up and frowned.

'Edward, *mon cher*, can you not find a less distracting means to divert yourself? My head aches with this noise.'

He swept the instrument to the floor in a show of sudden petulance. Anne looked up at him, the placidity of her expression hiding the contempt she felt for this discourteous boy who at times seemed unable to conquer his temper. He could be charming and considerate and there were other times when, like tonight, he seemed distrait, on edge. Soon his youthful voice would take on the shrill accent of some London fishwife and he would scream of his desire to join Warwick, and his father King Harry, put down further pockets of rebellion and punish the offenders.

Anne sighed. On these occasions she could well imagine that what one courtier had said of him was true, that he was a spoilt brat who talked of naught but war and cutting off men's heads.

At last Margaret rose to seek her own bed and Marian and Anne were free. They each swept a sedate curtsey and then went to Anne's chamber. She was silent as Marian helped her undress and she slipped naked into the great bed, where still she slept alone.

'Will Ralf go directly to Duke Charles's court, Marian,' she said at last, 'or do you think he may try to see you again?

'I hope not indeed.' Marian was vehement and she gave a tired smile in answer to Anne's candid gaze of unbelief.

'I shall not breathe till I know he is safe. The archer will bring me word. Praise God King Edward sails soon . . . ' She broke off as Anne's expression had darkened. Fool that she was she would have bitten through that prattling tongue of hers, rather than remind Anne that Edward's triumph could not be accomplished without the defeat of her father, but Anne had turned away and when Marian drew up a stool to sit by her bed, as she often did, she was insistent that she leave her alone.

'Go to your own bed, Marian. Read Ralf's letter in peace. I shall be well enough now.'

Marian extinguished all lights save one rushlight on a table near the bed. This she always left alight so that Anne might read from her psalter when sleep evaded her, then she gratefully withdrew.

The castle was quiet as she crossed the corridor to her own small chamber. Queen Margaret had been late retiring and most people had by now sought their beds. A sleepy page scrambled awkwardly to his feet as she passed. Some inconsiderate noble had kept the lad awake. Marian smiled. He was scarce more than a child. A smothered giggle from inside the room told her the reason for the boy's late vigil. His master was undoubtedly within with one of the French Queen's young ladies.

Marian's room was situated in the tower at the far end of the corridor and she was grateful that it was quiet and that she did not have to share it with others, though at times she found its distance from the Lady Anne's chamber somewhat inconvenient. Now, tired though she was, she could read Ralf's messages in peace and security.

She took a rushlight from a chest in the corridor, kindled it at a torch high above her head, and pushed open her own door. Lifting the rushlight holder to kindle another light of her own on an iron holder near the door, she turned to push the heavy wooden bolt into place. Before she could lift her arm to do so, she was seized from behind and her cries stifled by the calloused palm of a male hand.

'Steady, steady, my beauty. The boy in the corridor is tired but not so weary that he won't come at your call.'

Her eyes widened in terror, then she gave a great sob of relief as in the rushlight's uncertain glow she recognised the tall figure of her husband. He released her immediately, steadying her body against his own as he laughed down at her.

She swayed, dizzy with relief, yet dismayed at his foolhardiness. He quietened her with a kiss.

'Sweeting, don't let us waste time with chiding. I know I risk myself. Are you not worth it?'

'No, Ralf,' she shook her head emphatically. 'Naught is worth such a risk. My father is within the palace — all the Lancastrian lords — and Giles Crosby.'

'Let us not forget Giles Crosby.' His voice was grim though his eyes still smiled. 'Tell me, my love, are any of these in the habit of visiting your chamber during the hours of night?'

'Of course not . . . '

'Then we have till dawn.' He reached up to remove her hennin, his fingers insistent as she sought to stay him, then she gave way and allowed the heavy waves of her red gold hair to fall free onto her shoulders while his fingers swept through them and his eyes grew soft at the silken splendour of them.

'Ralf, I'm afraid.'

'Love, do you think I would endanger you?' His expression mocked at her fear. 'You are too valuable. Should you be caught with me, you will be safe enough. Your father needs you as pawn in his game. Only through you can he bind Crosby to him.'

'You think . . . ?'

'Aye, love. Become a widow and see how long before your father insists on your betrothal to Crosby.'

'Then for this reason you must not stay.'

His lips touched the top of her red-gold head and he lifted her high into his arms.

'Nay, lass, I know the price of folly. Can you truly ask me to go when it has been so long?'

Another sob was his answer and she lay still, no longer pleading when he undressed her then divested himself of his own stained travelling clothes.

Despite her agony of fear her body

surrendered to his, her passion rising to meet his own, until at last she lay content in his arms, one hand lifted to the sweat-dampened curls at his temples.

'You torture me, my love,' she whispered at last. 'God, how I long to come to you. You tell me I must not, but I'm your *wife*, Ralf, surely . . . '

'Love, I meant what I said. It is not possible. Perkin smuggled me inside.' He gave a little yelp of laughter. 'Louis takes less care over security than I dreamed possible, or his captains do. I entered at the gate with Perkin, went to the men's quarters, then later, when most were dining in hall, he brought me to the corridor.'

'But the page?'

'Gave me barely a look.' He bent to kiss the white roundness of her breast. 'You may lose your pure reputation, my Marian. His expression showed boredom, naught else. His life here is seasoned with engagements in the lists of love.'

She chuckled. 'I am not surprised. These French ladies are scarcely discreet. But how will you leave?'

'As I entered. I shall not be the only gallant to steal from my lady's chamber as the cold light of dawn tinges the sky. Don't concern yourself. Perkin will see me safe — if not?' He shrugged. 'I'm not ill used to danger, or did you think me some soft-living laggard, as Simon believed?'

'Where *is* Simon? Did he come with you?'

'Of course. He waits in my lodging, disapproving as ever, but he's reliable.'

'He hates me.'

'No. He feared that my love for you will betray us.'

'And he is right.'

'Tush, love. I cannot be expected to think of my squire's feelings.'

'You *will* leave Paris, tomorrow?'

'This very morning.'

She snuggled close as his words touched the pain of his going. For his own safety, she would have him go, yet it was sweet to lie close in his arms.

'Ralf, you are close to young Gloucester, I hear.'

'Aye, the lad trusts me at last.'

'What we heard — that he loves this serving woman, it is true?'

'Alys, the Duchess's maid? She has borne him a son.'

'Then he *does* love her.'

'Gloucester loves Anne Neville. You know that well enough.'

She was silent and he leaned over in the faint light to watch the shadow touch her lovely face.

'What is it?'

'Whatever you said to her, there is no hope. You know it. Her heart breaks for him, Ralf.'

'If Edward should die, she would then be free.'

'Die — young Lancaster?'

'He is mortal.' She flinched at the cold brutality of Ralf's tone. 'There will be more necessary blood-letting before England lies at peace again. Harry cannot rule, Marian. He is a puppet under Warwick. When he was brought from the Tower he mumbled and looked vacantly about him. 'Tis said he has scarce the wit to cleanse himself of his own night filth. England *needs* Edward and she'll not lie quiet while Harry or his heir lives.'

'Edward would execute the poor King and this boy?'

He turned abruptly from her, his eyes glinting at the note of sick horror in her voice.

'Answer me, Ralf. Would you have hand in such bloody work — and Gloucester. What does he say?'

'Young Gloucester is the King's right hand. He is no milk sop. He will do what is needed, as I shall be prepared to obey orders when the time comes.'

He had drawn from her, as though her horror had erected some invisible barrier between them, then abruptly he turned back and reached out for her. For one second it seemed she would resist him, then she gave way, and was his, compliant, responsive once more.

Just before dawn she felt him move from her. She reached out to stay him, then drew back her hand. It was time. He must go from her. She heard the clink of his harness, then he came to the bed and bent to give the kiss of parting.

'You know well I must leave you. It will take all my skill and cunning to get safe to Burgundy. You understand?'

'Yes.' Her little sigh was hardly audible, then she froze immobile, as her ears caught the measured tread of boots outside her door. His hand made a gentle pressure on her shoulder, cautioning her to keep calm.

The footsteps halted. They both waited, then a scratching on the door made her heart leap in sudden pain.

'My lord, you must come soon now.'

Ralf relaxed. ''Tis Perkin. Pray for me, love. My mother is well and waits to greet you soon again at Compton.'

He was gone. She felt him go from her, heard only the faintest betraying click of the door bolt, then she strained

296

her ears for what seemed hours, while she feared a sudden shout or scuffle which would tell her he was taken. A shudder went through her at thought of the consequences. Her father would take no chances. She doubted that he would even allow Ralf to live long enough to be tortured by Margaret's captains for news of March's force. Even the Queen's cause could not come before his need to rid himself of his daughter's unwanted husband.

At last she relaxed. He was safe. She felt it in her heart — or at least he was now. In the future, risking himself at Edward of York's side — that uncertainty must come later.

Now she was strangely comforted. Could it be that Ralf had sown his seed within her at last? She would pray to the Virgin day and night without ceasing. When first her father had removed her from Compton she had hoped for a child. To bear Ralf's heir would have been her triumph, but her hopes had been cruelly disappointed.

Was she barren? God could not be so hard. Even were Ralf to be taken from her, to have his child would assure her of victory over Crosby. Should she, in the last extremity, be forced to wed him, and the thought filled her with cold revulsion, he would not be entirely successful in his hopes. Ralf's child would inherit Compton and the bulk of her fortune. Her husband had risked much tonight, but by God's grace he might yet have achieved more than he knew.

16

Wearied beyond thought Marian waited in the kitchen while a young novice warmed some milk for herself and Anne. The girl's hands were trembling and Marian gave a wry twist to her lips as she noticed them. Poor child, well might she tremble. She was not like to remember such a day again.

'How is the Lady Anne?'

She turned to find Prince Edward leaning against the kitchen door behind him. He too was spent, she could see that. He had aged years seemingly in those hurried terrible days since they had landed. His pale face was strained but he seemed confident enough.

'She is bearing up. These last thirty-six hours of forced marching have well-nigh killed us all.'

He nodded, biting his lip and sinking wearily onto a rough hewn stool, while he watched the young novice at her task.

'The Queen seems better.' He shrugged. 'Now that the die is cast she is anxious for the outcome. Here at Tewkesbury we shall know one way or another.'

From the parlour Marian could hear the sounds of raised voices. Edmund Beaufort had insisted the Queen retire to this religious house, here at Gupshill, though she had preferred to camp with her army in the field near Holme hill.

'Madam, you will be safer here and you cannot abandon your other ladies to their fate. The prince will be in good hands.'

The swish of Margaret's travel-stained cloak could be heard as it swept the sweet new-lain rushes on the parlour floor. 'You know well, My Lord Duke, it is my custom to address my commanders.'

'God knows, madam, it is not my wish to prevent you. I myself will ride early tomorrow and escort you to the field, but stay here tonight and take your rest.'

The Queen's answer was not caught by Marian. The novice had given her the earthen pitcher of heated milk and she turned to pass the prince in the doorway. 'If you will excuse me, sir. I think this may help the Lady Anne to sleep.'

He nodded again and rose courteously, tired though he was. She bowed in acknowledgment and hurried on her errand. Strange how adversity could either improve or embitter a man. Since the news had reached them of Warwick's defeat and death at Barnet on the very day Margaret's army landed in Weymouth, he appeared to have thrown off his childish moods and was determined to prove himself a true son of Lancaster. Was it only three weeks since they had landed? It had been mid-April then and the Spring hardly advanced. Now the may was thick on the hedges. The bright sun had called out the white blossom early. In the orchards of the Cotswold hills the pear and apple were coming to bloom. All nature seemed to be reaching perfection of living, yet for many of their archers, billmen and pikemen out there in the field the local people called the Gastons it would be the last time they would see it. Edward's army had been sighted. The final issue would be settled in the morning.

Anne was lying flat on the hard little bed in the infirmary cell the nuns had put at her disposal. She sat up at once as Marian paused in the doorway. She was pale and wearied, as they all were, but there were no tears left. They had all been shed when news reached them of her father's death.

Poor Anne, without the comfort of her mother's arms or her sister's company, for Isobel was in her husband's train and he had returned to his allegiance. Persuaded partly by letters from Edward and more urgently by his younger brother, Gloucester, he had come to Edward near Banbury.

Kneeling gracefully in the dirt of the road before the King's tent, he had begged for pardon. Freely Edward had forgiven him yet kept him close on that Easter Day in the final bout with Warwick.

Now Anne's father and her uncle, Montecute, lay on two black draped biers before the high altar of St. Paul's, that Londoners might view for themselves the fall of the dread Kingmaker. Fog had enshrouded the field of battle and in the confusion Oxford's knights, who had pursued Hastings' left wing as far as Barnet and returned to the fray, were mistaken for the King's men. Somerset had attacked, believing the star on their banner to be the King's sun in splendour. It had cost Warwick the victory, and pale terrified King Harry, patiently awaiting the outcome, had been taken by Edward's men and now remained secure in the Tower once more.

The Countess of Warwick mourned at Beaulieu but Anne wept surrounded by Margaret's force with only Marian's gentleness for comfort. There was little from the Queen. Margaret stormed hysterically and had at first determined to return to France. Somerset had over-ruled her and for once young Edward refused to listen to her pleas. He would stay and fight, he said, and here at Tewkesbury in a vain endeavour to put the Severn between her and Edward's army, Margaret was forced to remain and fight.

Marian placed the pitcher down on a stool and poured warm milk into a rough earthen cup.

'Drink this, Anne. If you insist you cannot eat, this will help you to sleep.'

Anne reached out for the cup unprotesting, though she shook her head at Marian's insistence. 'Very well, to please you.' She sipped obediently. 'Come and rest too. Have some of this. Your need is as great as any of us.' She froze suddenly, the cup half way to her lips, as she saw her friend sway and stumble clumsily. For a moment Anne thought she would fall. She put down the cup, spilling the milk in her haste, and placed her arms steadyingly round Marian's shoulders.

'Come, Marian, lie back on the bed. You're faint. I'm not surprised. You're exhausted and you fuss too much over me. There was no cause to go down to the kitchen.'

Marian sank back gratefully against the hard pillow of the infirmary cot, while Anne removed her hennin and chafed her cold hands. For a moment the whitewashed walls of the bare cell had appeared to blur and dissolve before her eyes. Gradually the dizziness receded and she opened her eyes to find Anne regarding her anxiously.

'It is nothing. Don't be concerned.'

'You are ill. I know it, Marian. You will conceal these things. Let me ask for the sister who cares for the sick. She will have experience and . . . '

'No . . . ' Marian caught at her hand almost angrily. Anne stared at her, amazed at her vehemence, then down at the scratch where Marian's nails had drawn blood in her anxiety to prevent her from summoning assistance.

'I shall be well enough, truly.' Marian gave a tired smile.

'Marian, if there is something wrong you must trust me. You are no frail girl to faint with weariness. I know today has been gruelling, but I have watched you — you *are* ill.'

'No, Anne. I'm to have a child. My weakness is natural enough.'

Anne's lips parted soundlessly and Marian reached up one hand and gently drew her friend down to sit beside her on the bed.

'Don't look so shocked. This is Ralf's child.'

Anne drew a sudden startled breath and Marian nodded emphatically. 'He came to me that night after we saw him in the arbour.'

'Into the palace? But . . . '

'I know. It was utter madness. I said so. I begged him to go but,' she paused and flushed hotly, 'I loved him so. I wanted him, Anne. We needed each other and so he stayed.'

'Then you are four months gone with child, but why . . . '

'Why didn't I trust you? Oh, Anne, do not think hardly of me. At first I feared that any unwary word might betray his presence in Paris. I had no word when he left the city and even afterwards I feared pursuit. Later — when I first knew, I wished to keep my secret from my father.'

Anne pressed for no further explanation. She sighed heavily. Marian was not the first woman of her acquaintance to carry a child in adversity. When Anne had been only fourteen she had watched helplessly while Isobel bore a dead child, thrashing in agony in the fetid cabin of her father's ship off Calais. It seemed no miracle that Marian had somehow carried her child in safety during this terrible marching from Dorchester to Cerne Abbey then on to Bristol. At Gloucester they had found the garrison fortified by Sir

Richard Beauchamp's men and Margaret's company had turned back to Tewkesbury. Almost a month of continued marching. No wonder Marian was at the end of her reserves of strength.

'Thank God we are here in this nunnery,' she said quietly.

'I feared the Queen would insist that we camp with the army. At least you are safe here in Sanctuary.'

'Aye, the Queen is with the Duke of Somerset. Prince Edward asked after you.'

'How *is* he?'

'He will do well, I think, tomorrow.'

Anne's lips trembled. 'Marian,' she whispered, 'what hope is there for any of us? If Lancaster should win . . . ' She gave a great sob, '*Can* we defeat Edward's force? Is it possible?'

'Somerset is confident, though Pembroke has not brought the Welsh reinforcements he hoped for.'

'If we lose . . . ' Anne's terrified whisper brought Marian to sit suddenly upright and comfort the frightened girl.

'Edward is no monster. You will be safe enough. He does not make war on helpless women.'

'My father was a traitor to his cause and I — I am wedded to his enemy. What *will* he do to us if — if — we are taken?'

'Anne, you must pray for God's help. Whatever occurs in the morning we are in His hands. All these terrible hours today, I have told myself, Ralf is out there, I know it. Had he fallen at Barnet, I would have known. There would have been no need for messengers. He will help me, if he can, and Gloucester will aid you. Whatever happens you must believe that.'

During the night Marian lay on a truckle bed which had been forced into the small space of the cell that she might remain with Anne, but sleep evaded her, despite her bone weariness. For long hours Anne had prayed with the Queen before the high altar in the chapel. For once she had been firm in her refusal to allow

Marian to accompany her. For what each woman had prayed, in her extremity, Marian could not know. Here in the darkness she made her simple plea for her husband's safety on the morrow. He must live and know that at last she would give him an heir. He could not be snatched from her — not now.

At first light Queen Margaret was up and hurriedly dressed by her ladies. Anne and Marian accompanied her to Mass in the chapel. In the grey light of dawn the Queen looked haggard and old. Until this moment, Marian had not recognised that she was no longer a young woman, with the ability to hold men to her cause by her vibrant beauty and the force of her compelling personality. In her eyes Marian read the sick fear that she might lose her only son and her final hope in this coming contest, but when she left the nunnery, riding with Edmund Beaufort, she lifted her head in the old arrogant way and not once did she turn back to the quiet fair-haired girl in the doorway.

Anne turned back into the convent. She had made her farewell with her young husband the previous night. Marian had not asked what each had said to the other. She understood, in part, Anne's pain. Loving Richard of Gloucester as she did with her whole soul, she could not but pray for Edward's victory, yet if her young lord were slain, she would mourn him sorely. Despite his youthful arrogance, his boasting, and at times his wilful neglect of her at his mother's bidding, there had been times when he had taken her part. During these last days she had glimpsed the Edward of Lancaster there might have been had circumstances been different, or if he should gain the victory.

She seated herself in the small parlour with Marian for company, occupying herself with the skilful repair of a torn altar cloth. The light was stronger now. Both women lowered their heads to the task, their fingers moving mechanically, ears strained for the first sounds of conflict from the field.

When the Queen returned she withdrew into the chapel. She had quitted the field after addressing her commanders. Lord Wenlock was to take the centre and with him was the young prince. Marian privately wondered if this was a wise move. Wenlock had been an avowed Yorkist. For the white rose he'd fought at Towton. Now he was entrusted with the very life of the Lancastrian heir. Somerset was to command the right wing and Lord Devonshire the left. Marian did not discuss the coming battle with Anne. Tacitly each kept silent on the subject as if to put it into spoken words would intensify the fear each had about the outcome.

Marian's own fears were very real. She had had no news of Ralf. Had he survived Barnet? She had no way of knowing yet her heart told her he still lived. Her own father had taken leave of her the previous day and spent the night with Crosby on the field. They had parted without warmth. She had allowed Sir Humphrey to implant one cool kiss upon her brow. Crosby's quiet confidence disturbed her more. This smiling gentleman appeared to dread no reversal of his fortune. Could it be that he had made plans for his own prosperity whatever was the outcome?

The nunnery was rife with rumour, though the reverend mother forbade gossip. The nuns gathered in corners, gazing at their distinguished visitors from the corners of their eyes, or from lowered lashes as they scurried about the convent duties. Yet still Marian caught disjointed fragments of their chatter. King Edward's men were tired. They had already fought one campaign. The Queen had deliberately deceived his scouts by sending out detachments to Chipping Sodbury, as a feint towards London. Equally the Queen's forces had been exhausted by their days of marching and were disappointed that they had not been joined by Pembroke and his Welshmen. Both sides knew instinctively that on today's battle the hopes of white and red rose depended. The morning wore on, while the sound of cannon fire disturbed the peace of the religious house set in the heart of the Gloucestershire countryside.

To Marian, afterwards, there seemed no surprise when she saw Sir Giles Crosby ride to the convent door. She knew well enough that the battle was not yet decided. The noise of it could still be heard. She had left Anne in the parlour and gone to the kitchen for food. Common sense told her there would be little time for such mundane matters as the day advanced. Both the royal women would refuse it, she knew that too, but hoped to persuade them to break bread with some cheese or perhaps drink a cool draught of milk.

That at least would sustain them for whatever was to come.

As she crossed the entrance hall she saw Crosby. The portress admitted him, though nervous of his errand. He stripped off his gloves and stood hesitant before Marian. For once he was not smiling. His gravity touched her heart with an icy hand.

'Well, sir.' She gave him no time for polite evasions.

'It is you I seek, Lady Marian. Your father is gravely wounded. We have carried him to one of the cottages in Tewkesbury near to the mill.'

'You have left the field? How goes the battle?'

He shrugged impatiently. 'I had thought you would be more greatly concerned for your father. It is still undetermined. The prince has attacked and the Yorkists fell back. Somerset has attacked Gloucester's rear but his own flank was assailed by some two hundred spearmen Edward of York had placed in a wood to his right. As I helped carry your father to the baggage wagons, Somerset was undoubtedly relying on Wenlock to aid him — but will you come to Tewkesbury? If I can leave your father in capable hands I can return to the field.'

Marian turned towards the parlour but Crosby leaned forward and touched her on the arm. 'I have sent my squire to the Queen's grace in the chapel. He will carry my report. The Lady Anne will understand why you leave without word.'

She nodded and one of the nuns brought her a long cloak of fustian to cover her velvet gown.

'You will be less noticeable, my lady. We have such rough cloaks here to cover us when we attend the sick in the town. It is warm still, but your father may have need of it.'

Marian thanked her gratefully. It was true that her gown made her conspicuous, travel-worn though it was, as one of the Queen's ladies. She took off her hennin and pushed her hair under the hood attached to the grey cloak.

'Let us go, Sir Giles,' she said quietly.

He had brought her a palfrey and they rode the short distance in silence.

She looked about her anxiously but there was naught to see. No man was abroad and as they entered the town all the houses and shops were barred and shuttered. A little band of women was collected apprehensively near the main door of the Abbey. They muttered uneasily as Sir Giles passed with Marian. He assisted her to dismount in a small courtyard and stood aside for her to follow him into the little house. It bore a desolate air, as if no one had lived in it for some time. Weeds grew rank between the cracks in the stones of the court and there were cobwebs across the lintel of the heavily studded door. Crosby apologised for its state.

'It was the only place I could find. A woman from the next cottage supplied me with a key. I had no wish to break in. I paid her well. It was necessary. Your father cannot survive on the field.'

'How bad is it?' At last she gave her anxiety words.

'He received a crushing blow to the side of his head. One of Hastings' knights struck at him. Fortunately I saw the encounter. He fell from his horse. I was able to stand over him and pull him clear but I fear one leg is broken. I had two pikemen bring him here.'

As he pointed to the upper floor, she drew back frowning.

'The downstairs rooms are uninhabitable, the floor covered with filth. We carried him to the one possible chamber at the head of the stair.'

As he stepped back for her to mount before him, she noted he was not wearing armour. The fact had escaped her notice in the haste and anxiety of her departure, but now seemed not the time to comment. She had reached the top stair and hurried forward to fumble with the latch. Crosby put out an arm from behind and threw open the door. She ran forward with a little cry, 'Father . . . ' then stopped dead. The room was stacked with bales and chests but it was empty of any living soul. She swung round to find Crosby smiling gently, his back to the door.

'Forgive me, Lady Compton, but you would not have left the Lady Anne without good cause. I was forced to lie.'

She launched herself at him in a fury.

He adroitly caught her hands in his own strong ones, laughing at her animal-like pants of frustrated passion. 'Come, my lady, you will hurt yourself. At least allow me one moment to explain.' He released her abruptly and she staggered, almost falling in the suddenness of the impetus.

'That's better.' He pointed to a locked chest by the far wall. 'Sit down. Be sensible. Two of my men are below. You can do nothing, so why not listen to what I have to say in tolerable comfort.'

She backed from him, so angered by her stupidity in believing him, that for the time she could find no words to berate him. She shook back angry tears and said at last, 'Why — just tell me why?'

He smiled again, the maddeningly calm smile which she had first found so engagingly honest. 'I see you note I am not in armour. I am not such a fool as to trust myself in conflict. There is too much danger, my lady, as your father will doubtless discover for himself. The Queen has done me the honour to regard me as messenger. I find such a position, shall we say — convenient for my purpose.'

'And that is to save your own skin.' Marian's tone was withering.

He bowed without a trace of anger. 'Exactly, but not without profit. All you see here, my lady, is your own.' He waved his hand from the chests to the bulky packages. 'Silks, brocades, cloth of silver and, in the chests, ready gold from the shop in the Chepe.'

She stared at him unbelievingly and he nodded. 'But yes, I assure you. It is all legally yours. Your father and I have taken the trouble to have it conveyed here and stored for future eventualities. Of course,' his lips twitched, 'I do not think that he intended the same use for it that I have. He is over-anxious for the

Queen's cause.' He shrugged. 'I grant you, he is loyal to his own interests. If the Queen loses she will need capital for her escape and future needs. Now, I, I think that would be a waste. You and I can use the gold more fittingly.'

'If my father heard you speak now he would run you through where you stand,' Marian said slowly. 'God, if he knew you as I have known you.'

'It is strange, Lady Marian, that men like your father have uses for men like me and appear to fall into the error of regarding us as mere tools, to be trusted and then discarded when the need arises. They are blind to the fact that men like me have their own needs and are wise enough to plan for them.'

She stared at him for a moment, but even beneath her blazing contempt he did not lower his eyes.

'Well,' she said weighing her words carefully, 'you have told me so much. My goods are to be appropriated but why the need for me, Sir Giles? I confess the reason to acquire my person escapes me.'

A curious light sparked in his eyes and for one brief second only, his smile faded.

'You are strangely obtuse, Lady Marian. I want you. I have always wanted you. It is plain enough.'

'You will have me ride away with you now. Is that it?'

He bowed his agreement. 'There you have it. I am not disappointed in you, my dear Marian. You are a sensible lass. Why should we stay? Life could become acutely unpleasant for both of us. If King Edward is triumphant, and I have every reason to believe he will be, we are like to be arrested and indicted for high treason. Since I have not your exalted rank, that could mean disembowelling for me and the block for you, if indeed you are not condemned to the stake. You were not a countess when you assisted me in the attempted murder of the King and I think the sentence might apply to your status at the time of the crime. At all event, I do not think we should take risks. It is true I would prefer to have you bound to me by a gold band, but if not, then I am not base enough to abandon you. In Burgundy or Flanders we could live very well, don't you agree?'

Marian turned like a trapped animal to the window behind her. She realised that it would be fruitless to bandy words with Crosby. She wrenched at the casement, then peering down as it refused to budge, found that it was held firm by two heavy planks secured across the outside.

'Come, Marian,' Crosby reminded her of her plight, 'you don't think I was stupid enough to allow that? Even could you have opened it, would you have risked the drop? It's considerable.'

This gave her pause. In the old days she might have waited until he left her and hazarded herself from the sill — now there was Ralf's child to consider. Even to attempt to fight Crosby or his men could endanger that fragile life within her. She must wait in the hope that something would happen to divert him.

'So we fly the field before we know the outcome,' she jibed. 'How gallant, sir. I congratulate you on your prudence.'

His grin was rueful but unashamed. 'Do not think to sting me to some foolish act by taunts of cowardice. I'm not so easily provoked, my lady. But in fact I *do* intend to await the outcome. Should the Queen be victorious there will be no need to leave England. She trusts me — and you will be a widow.'

He saw his thrust had gone home. She went white to the lips and he continued, 'Be assured I shall see that fact is definite.'

Now her limbs felt heavy and ice cold. In his eyes she read his purpose. Should Ralf escape the slaughter, Crosby would make sure he died, either on the block among the noble prisoners or on the field by the hand of Crosby himself or one of his minions.

'It will avail you less than you hope, Sir Giles,' she said quietly. 'I . . . ' she broke off as the diversion she had hoped for occurred. There was a sound of horses' hooves coming fast up the street, a snort and whinny then her father's voice bellowing from the court below.

'Crosby, where in God's name are you, man? Is the baggage loaded? The wagons are ready. I fear they're needed. The battle goes against us. The Queen and her ladies have been informed. She is fled towards Worcester.'

Crosby swore, an ugly scowl marring the pleasing aspect of his face. He jerked open the door behind him and Sir Humphrey Benford clattered up the stair and stood panting, his armour dented, blood seeping between the armour plates on his right arm. His face was marked with blood, sweat and smoke and he was breathing stentorously.

'God, man, why do you wait? Did you not hear me? Edward, God blast him to hell, is triumphant. Gloucester fought like a tiger against Somerset's force and those spearmen of Edward's turned the tide of the battle. While I stood near the Prince, Somerset rode up like a madman screaming for Wenlock's head. He, poor devil, stood amazed. In truth I think he held back his men to protect the Prince on the Queen's orders. Somerset cut him down with one blow of his mace. Wenlock fell and all hell was let loose. I tried to help His Grace but I could not. The centre division broke and fell back towards the river, while Gloucester's force charged, pursuing us to the brink. How I extricated myself I'll never know. Desperation to warn the Queen and take possession of this gold drove me to cut down all who sought to stay me. There's no help for those in the meadow. It's a massacre, I'm telling you, and Edward in no mood to grant quarter.'

He stopped abruptly as he saw Marian, her hair streaming over her gown, her eyes wide with horror at his account of the battle's progress.

'So you burdened yourself with my lass? Marian, I am relieved to see you. Your peril is great, but by the Saints, man, had you left her with the Queen she might have joined us later. Now she will delay us.'

'No, Sir Humphrey. She'll not do that. The pursuit will be towards Worcester after the Queen and the Princess of Wales, so-called. I'll to the south with Lady Marian. It's yet possible we may reach London. Once there we'll not be recognised. The King's men will be busied here for some time.' He gave a grim yelp of laughter. 'The headsman will be over-occupied. By the time he turns for home Marian and I with the gold will have taken ship.'

He called down abruptly, 'Simon, Rob, load these final chests and the silk. The rest must be left. One of you secure the baggage and bring round the horses.'

The two pikemen brushed by the group in the doorway, ignoring Marian who was leaning, spent with horror and weariness, against the wall.

'Then you leave the gold to me? You take Marian without guard?'

Marian roused herself to hear her father's puzzled question.

'You mistake me, Sir Humphrey. The gold goes with me. I'll not follow the Queen. If you've the desire to risk your head then we take leave of each other here.'

Benford gave a strangled oath and lurched towards him. 'You'll desert Her Grace now? I'll see you roast in hell first.'

'It's likely enough, Sir Humphrey — but not yet. Be sensible, man. Come with us to Flanders. Seek the Queen later.'

'Try to take me, Sir Giles, and see how much I delay you.' Marian stood up and faced them squarely. 'I'll betray you at the first inn. I will not go one yard willingly in your company.'

Crosby snarled back at her, 'Then lose your pretty head.'

'I think not, Sir Giles. The King is ever merciful to women, especially one who carries the child of one of his nobles.'

He turned sharply, came towards her and leaned forward so close that his face almost touched her own. She did not falter though there was a strange glitter in his eyes that she had never seen before. Slowly he let his gaze travel the length of her body. Still she would not flinch, though it seemed an age before either he or her father spoke.

'So,' Crosby said at last, and his words were breathed out heavily as if he had been running, 'you played the wanton at Louis's court while I thought you so virtuous.'

'You wrong me, Sir Giles. My husband is the father of my child.'

'You lie, woman.' One hand jabbed out viciously, his gloved palm catching her hard across the cheek. She reeled under the blow and fell back so that she sprawled in an ungainly heap across the floor. Still his fury was unabated and he bent over her, his fist doubled, this time, ready to follow his first blow.

He gave a cry, half of alarm, half of temper, as Sir Humphrey Benford caught his elbow and jerked him away from the prostrate girl.

'Do you dare so mishandle my daughter?' he roared, his fury now as great as his fellow conspirator's.

Marian remained crouched on the floor. She was terrified that Crosby would so harm her that she might lose Ralf's child. Her own father's defence of her came as a sudden shock.

'Let me go. Are you a witless fool?' Crosby was now thoroughly roused. 'Can you stand there and listen to her lies? How long since she saw Compton, man? Have some sense.'

Through the fog of fear Marian found her voice to appeal to her sire.

'Ralf came to me in the palace at Paris. I carry his child and no other's. If

Ralf should die, yet there will be an heir to inherit.'

Crosby wrenched himself free from Benford's hold, his face working with the unleashing of his tightly held-in passion.

'God damn you as a whore and a liar,' he grated and he kicked her so that she yelped with pain and wriggled away from him to cower against the far wall, in an attempt to protect herself from his attack.

Benford drew his sword and challenged Crosby to face him.

'By all the Saints, I've heard enough, leave her alone, man. Vent your spleen on me if you must. The Queen's Grace needs you and I find you here bullying a helpless girl, one of my own blood to boot.'

Crosby turned from Marian to face her father. 'What do you think I care for the Queen's lost cause? If you've any sense, which I doubt, you'll leave her to her fate and make all speed for the coast. As for the goods, they are mine.

Sweet Jesus knows I've schemed hard enough for them.'

'You'll ride now and leave the wagons to me.'

'No, Sir Humphrey.' Crosby's voice expressed contempt. 'The gold and the girl come with me, even though now I find I must burden myself with her unborn brat — Compton's or no.'

Benford's eyes blazed. He stripped off his steel gauntlet and slashed it across Crosby's white strained face.

'Foresworn and cowardly dog. You'll take no child of mine nor yet save your own skin at the Queen's expense.'

'Get out of my way, old man.' Crosby spoke now quietly, without rancour. He meant business and he would not hinder to bandy words with this fanatical Lancastrian lord.

'You'll not leave this house unless over my body, Sir Giles.'

Marian saw through the blur of her tears Crosby's smile of sheer sweetness. It was a travesty of a pleasantry, the smile of a friend to one whom he held dear.

'So be it, Sir Humphrey,' he said gently. 'If I must kill you, why then I must.'

Benford appeared even then to be unable to believe that this man meant exactly what he said. Marian saw him check, his eyes narrow in doubt, then he came on for the attack. Crosby wore his own shorter broadsword slung from a serviceable belt round his hips. It was a French weapon, lighter, well balanced, more deadly, than the heavy blade of the older man. He parried Benford's lunge with ease and the man stumbled across the lintel of the chamber and struggled to recover himself. Crosby yelled below to his men Rob and Simon to leave the baggage and come up here, then he waited almost contemptuously for his opponent to come at him again.

Marian pulled herself to her feet. Until this time she'd remained huddled against the wall. Now alarm for her father's life galvanised her to action. She was helpless to interfere but she watched, horrified, as her father's dogged struggle began. Crosby was so much the better fighter the affair was almost ludicrous. Benford had been trained to fight on horseback. On foot, tired and strained as he was, he had no chance at all. He slithered and panted as his more agile adversary pushed him remorselessly from the room entrance to the head of the stair.

A sound of heavy feet ascending told Marian that assistance was coming to Crosby. She burst from the room, her warning dying unspoken on her lips. The pikeman came up easily behind her father and tackled from the rear. Sir Humphrey gave an infuriated bellow as he found his arms caught in a stranglehold then the roar changed to a strangling gurgle as Crosby leaned lightly forward and lunged at the old man's throat above the gorget. Marian gave a shrill scream as for one second his body remained upright, then as

Crosby's man released him, her father fell backwards down the stairs, his armour making a series of dull clangs as the man stepped aside and it slid downwards to remain at a ghastly angle in the hall below.

She moved forward to follow, but Crosby caught her arm and pulled her back.

'Rob, find Sir Humphrey's horse. Bring it to the door.'

The man nodded and sped down the wooden steps, contemptuously pushing aside her father's sprawled body when it impeded him. Giles Crosby was still holding tightly to her wrist and she broke her petrified silence in a choking sob.

'It is useless,' he said softly. 'He cannot aid you. We must go. We have no time for niceties of mourning. The old fool brought his fate upon himself . . . ' He broke off abruptly as his ears caught the sound of muffled cheering then shouts. Rob called hoarsely from the foot of the stairs.

'Sir Giles, the King is entering the town. It's over. Can you hear the crowd acclaiming him?'

Crosby swore and moved to the window. He stooped to peer down over the heavy board which secured it, and looked into the street below.

'Come up here, Rob.'

The man obeyed him at a stumbling run.

'What's happening? Do you know?'

'The Duke of Somerset and other Lancastrians took refuge in the Abbey. 'Tis said the Prince was killed in the retreat. The Abbot will try to protect them as right of Sanctuary, but Edward will hang all Lancastrians fleeing from the field. We should go, sir, at once.'

'No.' Crosby gritted his teeth and frowned. 'To attempt to run now would invite pursuit. The Yorkist soldiers will loot in the town and round up any enemy stragglers. We wear no livery. It will be safer if we remain in the town. Are the wagons well hidden?'

'Aye, sir.'

'Then return to them the two of you and wait for me. I'll come to you tomorrow.' He grinned wryly. 'We'll leave the town while the executions are in progress.'

'Do you stay here, sir?'

Crosby had not released Marian and she remained quiescent in his grasp, realising the stupidity of attempting to fight the man.

'No, at least, not for the present. I've business in the town. I'm unlikely to be recognised.'

He looked down at Marian and smiled deliberately. Horror rooted her to the ground. She read his purpose in the smile. As he had said, no one would be like to stay him. Flushed with the delight of victory the soldiers would be all unwary. Crosby could walk the field unhindered, even approach the King. At such a time Edward might well be unguarded. And Ralf . . .

Marian gave an inarticulate cry and Crosby's smile widened.

'Do not fear, Lady Marian. You will

be perfectly safe here and tomorrow we can leave without haste. Who knows, perhaps by then you may be a widow.'

The pikeman looked at her unmoved as she swayed where she stood, sick with fear and sorrow.

'The woman will stay — in the house then?'

'Aye. You go about your business. Allow none to enquire too closely about the wagons. I may return here — tonight.' The pause before the last word was significant. He released her wrist abruptly and she fell backwards against the window. Before she could recover herself they were both gone.

She gave a wild cry and pounded at the barred door. Already she could hear the two men leaving the flagged hall. She screamed Crosby's name yet knew it was useless. She turned, leaning against the door to face the window. The noise in the street had built up. The crowd had come with the King and the victorious royal Dukes to the Abbey door. She could hear the massed roar and the noise of horses' excited whinnyings as the chargers were firmly held in by their riders. A woman screamed from below. Possibly some soldier had attempted to seize her.

Marian ran to the window and clawed at the thin horn which served to admit the light. Without a knife or dagger she could make no impression on the horn and it was impossible to open the casement. She hammered on the wooden support and screamed but the shouts and yells from the crowd below drowned out her cries and she gave up in the end, exhausted.

Oh God, what could she do? Her father lying dead in the hall below, the Queen fled, and she helpless to seek Ralf and warn him of Crosby's deadly spite.

Why should Giles Crosby seek to kill her husband at such a time when he himself was in such peril? It seemed pointless and yet she had read him correctly. In this terrible moment Marian understood the other's hate.

For some inexplicable reason he desired her, almost as much as he did her gold hidden in the wagons with his two henchmen. He had always wanted her from their first meeting in her husband's house. She had not considered him — no, she lied to herself, she had known he had found her not unattractive but she had overlooked him as a suitor. Ralf had come home and they had found fulfilment each in the other. Perhaps her very tendency to ignore Crosby then and later, when her contempt for him as a creature of her father's was made plain, had made him her deadly enemy. If he could not have her love, neither would Ralf. The fact that she carried Ralf's child added fuel to his hatred.

She covered her face with her hands and let her tired body slip to the ground and, sitting there with her back to the window, she gave way to despair and sobbed out her grief.

The noise from below grew in crescendo. She checked as she heard heavy blows from the street. Edward was at the Abbey door. He would demand that the traitors be given up to him. Marian shivered uncontrollably. God help Somerset now. Even her father had been spared the final indignity of the block.

She stifled a scream as she heard heavy steps ascending the stairs. She scrambled unsteadily to her feet. Had Crosby returned — so soon? The steps were unsteady, lurching and accompanied by a sound she could not identify. She backed to the wall again, her hand across her mouth in panic. Whoever it was had halted and there was a pause. Why didn't Crosby call out to her? Who was it out there?

She winced as the bolts squealed and the door was flung open. She had closed her eyes in her fear, then she opened them as a hoarse voice spoke her name.

'Marian, girl, you must go.'

'Father.' She screamed in shock as Benford reeled into the room. Blood smeared his breastplate and he could hardly remain upright. As he fell she gathered him into her arms, lowering his body to the floor.

It seemed impossible that he could live still. She had believed his windpipe severed by Crosby's thrust, yet he had accomplished the terrible climb up the stairs. Blood frothed from his lips and he mouthed up at her:

'I did not know ... the man ... was ... '

'Don't try to speak.' She rocked backwards and forwards in her agony of grief.

'I thought I could — use — him.'

She nodded and stooped to kiss the cold forehead.

'If you are found here it will mean the stake.' For this last desperate effort his voice gained power. 'Leave me now.'

She waited only a moment then as he gave a despairing wave of his hand she lowered his head and shoulders and moved to stand up.

Almost immediately he sighed, blood

bubbled up again and she saw that a bluish hue had tinged his lips. The eyes were glazing fast as she went to the door, turned back once to look her last at him, then plunged down the stairs and into the crowded street.

17

It was fortunate for Marian that the crowd in the street had gathered with but one object in view, that of determining if King Edward would obtain from the Abbot what he demanded, the handing over to him and his officers the person of Edmund Beaufort, Duke of Somerset, and the other Lancastrian lords, as they huddled in a blood-stained, dispirited heap under the soaring pillars of the Abbey. All eyes were on the Abbey door and the mood of the assembly was hushed after the excitement earlier. A woman near Marian sobbed aloud her grief.

'Poor lad, so young to die, and he was so badly disfigured. It was hard to tell who he was lying so on that bier.'

Another woman, much older, added her opinion. 'Aye, just seventeen, they say, young handsome prince and the apple of his mother's eye. Well, he'll have escaped the headsman's axe and that's some comfort.'

Marian stood stock-still for a moment. So Prince Edward was indeed slain and they had brought his body to the Abbey. So that was why the crowd had stilled so suddenly. She dashed a hand angrily across her eyes. So much death and destruction, would it never end? The first woman glanced at her, and she whispered urgently to her companion. Both then turned again and openly stared. Marian waited no longer but pushed her way into the thickest of the crowd. Too well she knew why she had attracted such attention. Her red-gold hair streamed loose from her hood, her velvet gown was dabbled with her father's blood and torn where Crosby had handled her roughly. The cloak had suffered no less damage, but it served to cover the richness of her gown's material which marked her out as someone of note.

The Abbot was speaking quietly. Marian caught only the gist of his discourse. If the King would allow them the right to confess their sins and pray for their dead, on the morrow the Lancastrian lords would themselves emerge from Sanctuary. She had reached the fringe of the multitude now and she took to her heels and ran, back along the road towards Gloucester, towards Gupshill and the battlefield.

Exhausted as she was, she was soon halted by the need to stay by the wayside and catch her breath. A heel had come loose from her shoe of fine kid and in the end she stumbled along. It was getting dusk and there were few people to be seen. Ahead she could see the glimmer of camp fires and she knew she was approaching the field. To her right was the religious house where she had left Anne and the bereaved Queen. It would be useless to seek the aid of the nuns. They could not help her and she knew the two royal ladies had fled long since towards Worcester. No doubt they would be overtaken and brought back prisoners to Edward's camp before long. One urge drove her forward, panting and sobbing with the effort: she must find Ralf if he were yet alive and warn him of Crosby's presence in the vicinity of the town. Every other thought had vanished from her mind, even the knowledge that to deal so harshly with her own body might lose her Ralf's child.

Near the baggage wagons a group of camp followers were busied about the fire. One of the women stood up as Marian passed and called some bawdy comment that at any other time would have brought forth a red flush to her cheeks. The lurid glow of the camp fire made the woman appear like a creature out of hell, with her dark locks waving in the evening breeze and the flames lighting up her bold, handsome features. Determined not to be kept from her search, Marian turned from the wagons and began to run. From somewhere behind the harlot, a man's voice called out to her in invitation and she heard the woman's screech of laughter which accompanied it.

To her left she saw the silken pavilions of the royal dukes and further off the King's tent with the royal standard of the leopards and lilies guarded by two stalwart pikemen. Near to Gloucester's tent Ralf would be quartered. It could not be long now before she could have the protection of his strong arms. One pikeman near the King's tent challenged her harshly and she came to a halt.

'What are you doing here, woman? Your place is with the wagons. Get back there.'

Marian hesitated. Indeed she must appear to this soldier a sister of the camp fraternity. Should she reveal her identity? To do so would render her liable to arrest. Who knows whether she was still under sentence?

The man frowned and advanced. She had made him no satisfactory answer and she had not given ground. He was determined to know more of her before allowing her to slip through his fingers.

'Did you hear me? This section of the camp is forbidden to all without passes. What do you want?'

'I seek Sir Ralf Compton's tent.' She looked up at him fearfully as his eyes took in the state of her clothing.

'Sir Ralf? Who calls him still by that mode of address? Don't you know, woman, you talk of My Lord Earl?'

'Of course,' Marian faltered but pressed on, 'I — I knew him before the King honoured him. Will you tell me how to find him? My business is urgent.'

'I don't know.' The man narrowed his eyes and gave a sigh of relief as the guard captain came within view. Marian restrained a startled gasp for the man was known to her. He had been in service with the King during his visit to Compton, had indeed been in charge of her by order of Lord Hastings.

'Captain,' her challenger asked for his assistance. 'This woman asks to see My

Lord Earl of Saxby.'

The captain seized a smoking brand from a holder outside the King's tent and strode forward. The flaring torch revealed to him Marian's terrified features and the stiffening blood stains down her robe. He started, recognising that red-gold hair immediately.

'Lady Compton? It is you?'

Marian nodded. It was useless to hide the fact. 'Captain, I must see my husband. He will keep me close until the King has leisure to order my situation — but please.'

The captain turned to his subordinate and spoke brusquely. 'This woman is a traitress. Secure her with the other prisoners for judgment in the morning. Be quick now, for the King will ride soon from Tewkesbury. He has supped with My Lord Abbot.'

As the guard seized her Marian struggled in a last desperate effort. 'Please — you must listen to me. Tomorrow will be too late. I cannot wait.'

The guard held her tightly and she was exhausted. He spoke kindly but firmly.

'Come, lady, we mean you no ill. In the morning the Duke of Gloucester will hear your plea. He is Lord Constable of England.'

Gloucester — of course. If she could be brought before the young Duke she could be sure of a hearing. She rallied her failing senses for a last appeal but as if in answer to an unspoken prayer the quietness of the camp was broken by sounds of return. A small troop of mounted lords swept up to the pavilions and the pikeman came instantly to attention.

'What is this?' A stern youthful voice Marian knew well questioned her captor. 'Do you arrest a looter so close to the King's tent?'

'My Lord Duke . . . ' Marian burst from the guard's hold and launched herself towards his stirrup. 'You must let me speak with you now. In the morning either Ralf or the King might be dead.'

Gloucester peered down at her uncertainly. He was still clad in his gilded armour but had removed his helmet. Behind him rode his standard bearer, Blanc Sanglier. His brown hair was damp with sweat and his features drawn with tiredness. He appeared to have aged at least ten years since last they'd met and Marian thought, with a pang, of the youth who'd courted Anne Neville with such grave sincerity. Now he was the King's right hand, Lord Constable of England and one of the realm's most noted commanders. She had heard that Barnet had been lost, to some extent, because of the prudence and gallantry of this young prince. But other things were said of him, that he was ruthless — unforgiving. Marian flinched under his direct regard.

'Lady Marian.' He signalled to the guard to stand back. 'I confess I had not thought to find you here.' He called to the attentive squire behind him.

'Piers, escort this lady to my tent and bring us wine.'

Marian was led away. She turned once to find the Duke had dismounted and was in urgent talk with his captains then the young man pushed aside the tent flap and she went inside. A hanging lantern lit the Duke's quarters. Quietly the squire invited her to sit upon a folding stool and prepared to pour wine from a pitcher on the table which also held a litter of maps, papers and a book of hours.

When Gloucester entered, she rose at once. He stripped off his steel gauntlets and gestured her to seat herself.

'Sit down, Lady Compton, you are exhausted. Take some wine.'

'But first you must listen. Crosby will murder Ralf. He said . . . he said . . . '
In her agitation she had dropped the wine cup and the spilt wine added to the ruin of her gown. She ran towards him, her fingers held out beseechingly, tears choking the words before she could utter them.

He caught her as she almost fell and conveyed her back to the stool, snapping his fingers urgently at his squire.

'More wine, Piers. Hurry, lad.' He took the cup and pressed the metal rim to Marian's lips sensing how close she was to utter collapse. 'Drink, Marian. Do not try to speak yet. I shall not leave you. You are quite safe.'

Once before someone had given her such comfort. She swallowed hard and found the wine course through her with fire and added strength. She coughed weakly then pushed gently against the hand which held the cup.

'My lord, I thank you. I am better, truly.'

'You can talk now?'

She nodded, biting at her lip to prevent the sudden attack of trembling from preventing her from answering his questions.

'You were with the Lady Anne?'

'Yes, in the convent at Gupshill.'

'Where is she now?'

'I do not know.' Marian turned from the anguish that clouded his grey eyes.

'I have been her attendant these many months since — since her father took her to Queen Margaret's court. I was with her this morning.'

'When did you see her last?'

'About noon I think it must have been. I had gone to the kitchen for food when Giles Crosby came. He told me my father was gravely wounded and needed tending in Tewkesbury. It was a lie but I believed it and went with him. He swore he had left instructions for the Lady Anne but I doubt that he told the truth after what followed. It is a long tale, my lord, and most of it does not concern you save that he and my father had gold in some wagons hidden in the town against the possibility of Queen Margaret's defeat. Crosby intended it for his own use and, when my father came with news of the Queen's flight, they quarrelled. He slew my father and, when he knew there was little chance of escaping the town, he left the house intent on murder.' Her words rose to a pitch nearing hysteria. 'I swear he meant what he said. He is wearing no armour or livery. He is not known to the King's men. He will seek out Ralf and kill him. I pray you take me to my husband.'

Gloucester had taken one cold hand within his own. He felt her claw at it in mute appeal and bit his own lip, uncertain how to answer her.

She drew back, staring into his stern face, then she whispered, 'Ralf, he is dead? Is that it?'

'We know not.' Gloucester took both her hands to stay her as she made a pathetic attempt to rise. 'No, Lady Marian, you must believe me. Ralf's squire has been searching for him. Until he returns and tells us he has found the body, we must not believe the worst.'

'Then he is wounded — lying out there . . . ' She broke off and gave way to terrible, racking sobs. If Ralf were gone what had she to hope for now, not even a protector in the King's camp?

'Almost certainly the Earl is wounded but he may yet recover. Come, Marian, time is still young. Many search for their wounded on the field. You must hope and pray.'

She conquered her tears as she realised the wisdom of his advice, then another fear touched her with an icy hand.

'There are others who search the field?'

'Aye, others who rob and kill. We mount a guard but there are always scavengers.'

'Then Crosby might yet kill Ralf.'

His grey eyes flashed as he understood her alarm. 'True. We must warn Wentworth. First, Marian, do you think Anne went with the Queen?'

'She could do nothing else since she is wife to Prince Edward.' Marian avoided the hurt in his eyes. 'My father said they were heading for Worcester. He hoped to follow with the gold but Crosby . . . '

'Aye, do not think of it. There will be time to mourn.'

She looked up at him, her tears over.

'I know it, Your Grace. I shall not be alone after this day. It is true that Prince Edward fell?'

'Aye, they carried him to the Abbey.'

'I heard as much. At least — I did not see it but the people were talking.'

Gloucester spoke urgently to his squire. 'Piers, go to the Earl of Saxby's tent and find his squire. Ask if there are tidings.'

'Sir.' The squire obeyed him and Gloucester reached for a cloak flung over his camp bed.

'Do not fret, Marian. Since this man Crosby might well be at liberty within the camp, I'll alert the King's guard to his danger and myself join in the search for Ralf.'

He frowned as his squire came hurriedly back. 'Well?'

'Sir, there is news of the Queen. I thought you would wish to know . . . '

'Admit my captain then go as I bade you.'

'Aye, sir.'

A man entered the circle of light. He

was fully armed and covered in dust. He had obviously ridden hard. He waited for no permission to speak. 'My lord, the Queen and the Lady Anne were overtaken by men in the Duke of Clarence's company. They are under guard awaiting the King's pleasure. Since the Lady Anne is the Duchess of Clarence's sister, he has offered her protection.'

'Damn him.' Gloucester's words were grated through closed teeth.

The elderly knight swept him one questioning glance from under bushy brows.

'I was too late to take command, sir. Is it your wish that I approach the Duke and . . . ?'

'No.' Gloucester turned to his work table, the set of his shoulders expressing complete soul weariness.

'Thank you, Jehan. You brought me word. You can do no more. I will see His Grace the King in the morning after our business at the Abbey is concluded.'

Marian caught her breath at his grim tone. This time there was to be no quarter. The adherents of the House of Lancaster must die. York must reign unchallenged. She could recall Ralf's words as she had lain in his arms in her small room in Louis's palace. The thought had filled her with sick dread. Now she was face to face with the reality.

So Anne was to be kept under the control of her brother-in-law. Marian could picture her mistress's utter despair. She had ever disliked Clarence and, since his betrayal of her father at Barnet, her antipathy had hardened into utter contempt. What kind of treatment could she expect at his hands when he treated his wife so shamefully?

The older man bowed and withdrew after giving Marian one cursory glance. Gloucester took up from the table a workmanlike dagger and strapped it into a small sheath suspended from the belt at his hips.

'We will wait for my squire. He may have news.'

She nodded. 'I am sorry about Anne, but Clarence will guard her well.'

He frowned. 'True, perhaps too well.'

'But why should he keep her from you? Surely she will be an encumbrance.'

'A very wealthy one.'

Marian turned away. Only too well she knew the truth of that fact. She swung round as Gloucester's squire re-entered the tent with a jingle of harness and spurs.

'Sir, Wentworth came back about an hour ago. His search had been unsuccessful, but he recently left again with two men carrying a bier. He was told that the Earl had been last seen in the press of the pursuit down by the river near the mill. When you called the retreat, apparently he did not follow. 'Tis said many of the Lancastrian knights drowned in the mill stream. Some of our men drew them out. The bodies lie thick on the bank. It may be . . . '

'Quite.' Gloucester cut him off short as Marian had gone paler than ever in the uncertain light in the tent. 'Accompany me, Piers. Cover your livery. I have no time to remove my armour, but this cloak will serve to hide it. Bring a torch and come armed.'

'Aye, sir.'

Marian pulled her hood hurriedly over her dishevelled hair and stood up.

Gloucester shook his head. 'You must wait here, Lady Compton. You can do naught out there. The field is no place for you.' His eyes flickered over her tired form. 'Certainly not in your condition.'

'You have sharp eyes, my lord. You are the first to notice.'

'When I held you and carried you to the stool it was obvious that you are with child.'

'It is Ralf's child, I swear it.'

He smiled thinly. 'I believe your word, lady, but it is better you stay. The sights in the field, particularly at this hour when the human vultures are abroad, are not pretty.'

'My lord, I have recently held my dying father in my arms. After that I can stand anything and it is imperative I go with you. I *know* Crosby; you do not.'

He considered while the squire waited attentively. 'That is so.'

'Crosby will recognise Simon Wentworth. He may follow — Simon is no match for Giles Crosby however well he is guarded.'

Gloucester moved a ring on his finger thoughtfully. His grey eyes scanned her face carefully then he jerked his chin once in agreement.

'Very well. There is wisdom in what you say. Stay close to me.'

Outside he spoke with one of the captains who saluted and went immediately to the King's tent. Gloucester set out purposefully, having decided against an armed guard. His squire was reliable and had already shown his mettle at Barnet. The two of them were a match for any attacker and there would be guards within call if they were needed. He preferred to search the field like any other private citizen. It was safer so. Round the tents the wounded had already been tended. Later they passed one or two more being assisted by companions or carried on litters. Other men walked silently, their arms full of friends' weapons or possessions. Gloucester headed for the meadow by the river, while the squire lighted his way.

Here a terrible sight awaited them. Marian would never recall the experience afterwards without a cold shudder of terror. The whole scene was like an illustration in some holy book depicting a landscape in hell. Flares carried by searchers picked out the heaps of the slain and as they passed they heard low moans, prayers and appeals for water. Once a kneeling woman rose from a stooping position as Piers held a torch high to reveal her hideous features and the filthy, talon-like fingers. Grey matted hair fell onto her shoulders and she drew her lips back in a snarl of rage as Gloucester snapped in a voice which allowed no disobedience, 'Get you hence, hag. Leave the dead to God. Go about your jackal task in some other portion of the field.' She staggered away with a low voiced curse and Piers gave a sudden exclamation as the torchlight caught the flow of new blood which issued from the corpse's throat.

'See, my lord, that devil slew a living man. Lancastrian that he was he deserved not to die by the hand of that ghoul.' Marian stumbled against Gloucester in a half-faint. The horror of the deed turned her sick. He gave a muffled cry and both she and Piers looked up at him in alarm.

'You are wounded, sir.' The squire turned from his perusal of the slain soldier to hold the torch up to look into his master's pale face.

''Tis nothing, lad. I was blooded in the shoulder. A surgeon dressed it soon after the battle. It will do well enough. Let us get on.'

Marian stumbled out an apology but he took her arm gently. 'Come, Lady Marian, let us waste no more time. This recent work shows us the need for haste. To cut the throats of the wounded to steal a weapon or jewel is not unusual at this hour. It is for this reason I wished to spare you. If we are to find Ralf alive we must be quick.'

She waited for no more but followed him eagerly. Their progress was difficult. The ground had been churned up by the men and horses and was slippery underfoot, whether with blood or recent rain, Marian could not tell. Once or twice she almost fell and was lifted to her feet either by the young squire, Piers, or by Gloucester himself. It was not difficult to tell which bodies to search. Two men only had their close scrutiny as they had worn armour. Both were dead. One's armour had been almost entirely removed by one seeking booty. The rest of the slain were either bowmen or pikemen in leathern harness. Even these had not been left in peace, but lay sprawled, half unclad and bereft of hoods or boots.

Near the river bank they encountered Simon Wentworth and his two archers. The squire's sullen features had become drawn with weariness and despair, his fair hair almost unrecognisable, sweat-streaked and blackened.

Gloucester hailed him and he sighed at his report. 'Wentworth, what news, man? My lord's wife seeks him.'

Wentworth eyed her warily, his expression half of distrust, half of curiosity.

'There is no sign of the Earl near the mill itself, sir. We have searched thoroughly. Many knights fell there, but not my lord. I am now going to take the right bank in a last search. If, indeed, he rode further towards the Abbey, it is strange we have no word of him.'

'Good, man. Lady Compton and I will cross at the ford and take the further bank towards the Gloucester road. It is possible he followed some personal enemy.'

Wentworth bowed his acknowledgment and Gloucester took Marian's arm to lead her towards the river crossing.

'The boy fought well and honours Ralf. I had thought him boorish and unknightly. I was wrong. Ralf spoke glowingly of his prowess at Barnet and he will win his spurs for his valour at both battles. If he can find Ralf, he will. He had not spared himself.'

Marian touched his arm fleetingly as she saw a slinking figure slipping along by the reeds on the near bank of the river.

'Another thief, my lord? He — he seems familiar.'

'Crosby?' Gloucester signalled to his squire to draw closer and to be silent. He himself whispered the word in her ear. 'Has he seen us?'

'I don't know. I think he has not. I am not sure. He has seen something in that patch of reeds.'

'He has indeed — a glint of armour dulled but unmistakable, something

Wentworth missed. Follow Wentworth, Piers, and bring him here, but quietly now. Give me the torch. You can follow the glow of Wentworth's. He is only yards away from us.'

The squire hurried off and Gloucester advanced, cautioning Marian to stay close. The thief had stopped by the water's edge. Marian could hear the distinct sound of the lapping of the water against the bank and her own audible breathing. Gloucester held the torch high as the man's back was turned towards them. The light glimmered on an upraised blade. Marian gave a startled scream. They were too far from the wounded knight to aid him, whoever he was. She heard a sudden hiss. The thief gave a scream of agony, rose almost to full height, then fell forward onto his victim. Marian turned to Gloucester as he gave a muttered bark of satisfaction and ran forward to follow the path of his own dagger.

He called imperiously to Marian to

stand back and caught the thief by the neck, dragging him clear. The man's own dagger had dropped harmlessly to the grass as Gloucester's dagger had found its mark in his unprotected back. Gloucester snatched it up. Marian caught a glimpse of Giles Crosby's distorted features, the pleasant smile drawn back in a grin of agony. That he still lived, she did not doubt. She hid her face while Gloucester ruthlessly stabbed upwards. When she turned back, the body of her father's killer quivered once and then lay still. Gloucester drew him clear of the body of the knight, who lay half concealed by the tall reeds. Marian crept close, too frightened to gaze on the man's face. Gloucester gently lifted clear the helm and gave an exclamation of concern.

'Come, lady, our search is ended. Here is Ralf.'

She scrambled to his side, staring down at her husband's white face. Even now she did not know — dare not ask. 'Is he . . . is he . . . ?'

'No.' Gloucester bent over him, listening intently. 'He lives but appears to have been unconscious for hours.' His eyes searched Ralf's body for wounds, then he reached out and felt at his head.

Marian touched Ralf's cold brow and stooped to kiss him.

Gloucester checked as Simon Wentworth and the three other men hurried to the bank.

'We must be careful, Wentworth. There may be brain damage.' Gloucester had already stripped off his cloak and wrapped it round the wounded man. Wentworth nodded then ordered the two men to place the improvised stretcher on the ground.

'Can we not try to rouse him first?' Marian looked upwards at the anxious faces of the men.

'That would be unwise,' Gloucester said gently. 'We'll get a surgeon to him. Take him to his tent, Simon. If the surgeon advises it, we'll convey him to permanent quarters in Tewkesbury later.' His eyes followed the others' to the twisted body of Giles Crosby.

'A looter who saw the chance of valuable armour, most likely,' he said briefly. 'It was lucky I caught him before he struck.'

Simon Wentworth stooped over the dead man, looked towards Marian then at the Duke, shrugged, then stood back while the two archers lifted their burden with utmost care and the little party made its way towards the King's encampment.

While the King's surgeon examined Ralf, Gloucester drew Marian outside the tent. She was reluctant to leave Ralf but he insisted.

'Give him a chance to examine him thoroughly. Simon is in attendance.'

He looked across the field to where, in daylight, the Abbey tower could be seen from the town.

'It seemed a foolhardy action to seek out Ralf Compton. It *was* Crosby, without doubt?'

'Yes.' He eyed her curiously as she

caught back a sigh. 'You had some feeling for this man? You knew him well at Margaret's court. Naturally you regret his death?'

She gave a little shudder. 'He tried to kill Ralf from pure spite and hatred. I regret any man's death but Crosby was spawned in hell. On the surface he was translucently honest, beneath . . . ' She broke off. 'He spied on me for his own reasons and when Lady Anne and I sent a messenger to you he followed and murdered him. He read the messages and saw fit to give them to my father and to the Earl of Warwick. The Lady Anne paid dearly for her part in it. He embroiled me when he attempted to poison the King. He was paid spy and murderer and, even in that, he could not remain faithful to his paymasters. He stole my gold and deserted the Queen, when, God knows, she had most need of him, then my father — you know of that?'

'He took a grave risk simply to kill Ralf?'
She coloured and avoided his gaze. 'I

think — I think in his way he loved me. I gave him no encouragement but this was his reason. I cannot say why. I am an heiress, of course, as you yourself said, my lord. No man cares for me for myself alone.'

'Nay, lady, you count yourself of too little worth. Ralf loves you. Why do you think he risked himself in Paris?'

The surgeon emerged from the tent and Gloucester led Marian forward.

'How is he?'

'It is difficult to say, My Lord Duke. Until he regains consciousness I cannot assess the extent of the injury.'

Marian's alarm deepened. 'He will recover?'

'Yes, lady. The Earl will live but . . . ' he spread his hands in a deprecating gesture, 'if the brain is damaged he may not be himself,' he ended somewhat lamely, his expression pitying.

'You mean he may not be sane?' The last word was so low it was clear that she could hardly bring herself to utter it.

'He may not know you, or remember the past or even walk or function normally. I cannot hide from you the gravity of such a condition. You must be prepared for it.'

'When — when shall we know?'

Again the surgeon spread his hands wide. 'We must wait. It may be hours — or days. Nature takes its own time, often executes its own cure in these cases.'

Inside the tent Ralf lay silent and still on the narrow camp bed. Simon Wentworth rose from a stool at his side and made way for Marian. She sat down and took Ralf's limp cold hand in her own. She felt, rather than saw, Simon leave the tent. She sat on through the remaining dark hours and through the cold grey light of dawn. Later the noise of men stamping on the chilled ground and the renewed crackling of fires told her the camp had awakened. Simon Wentworth brought her bread, meat and ale but she could not eat. Her whole life was concentrated on this watching of the beloved face.

Then towards noon Ralf stirred. Marian caught her breath, rose and bent over him.

'Ralf, my dear love. Come back to me. It is I, Marian.'

He gave a strange grunt and settled back again into semi-stupor.

Marian choked back a wild sob of panic. 'Ralf, my husband, I have waited so long to tell you that I carry your child.'

He stirred again as though her voice had penetrated to his consciousness engulfed in the mist of sleep or stupor, which, she could not tell. His lashes flickered and to her joy she saw his eyes open. They stared unseeing at the tent roof, then his fingers clutched at hers and he turned his head, but slowly, oh so slowly.

She waited in an agony as his clouded brain sought to discover his whereabouts and situation then he looked full at her and his lips parted in the ghost of a grin.

'Marian, you here?'

'Yes, my love. Lie quiet. There is naught to fear. The King is victorious.'

His expression told her nothing. He gave no indication of having understood her tidings. A cold knot tightened in her stomach. He knew her, and could move some of his limbs, it was true, but had he realised the implication of what she had told him? She feared not. There was no reaction. He gave a tired smile and, just as suddenly, relapsed into sleep again.

Some hours later the King visited the tent with Gloucester. He treated Marian with grave courtesy and assured her he regarded her as cleared of any accusation made against her.

'He seems long coming out of this,' he said quietly, regarding Ralf with concern.

'He knows me, sire, but I doubt if his brain functions normally yet.'

'Oh?'

'I told him I was carrying his child. He expressed no joy or surprise.'

'I see.' The King pursed his lips,

nodded and left the tent with his brother.

When Simon Wentworth brought her supper, she forced herself to eat though, even then, her eyes hardly left Ralf's face. The squire avoided her gaze as though he, too, feared the worst.

Towards evening Ralf's eyes flickered open again and she brought him wine and water at his muttered request. He drank deeply and then lay back regarding her steadily.

'Are you in pain, my love?'

He shook his head only slightly, but still there seemed little awareness of the crisis through which they had all passed. She went to the tent door and called for some meat broth. He ate obediently and without coaxing. Afterwards she sat quietly on the stool at his side while he lay peacefully like a child. Suddenly he said, 'All is well with you?'

'Yes. Do not concern yourself about me.'

'It is good.' Again he lay quiet then he chuckled but slightly so that she jerked upright with the wonder of it.

'I regret you have had problems to explain your condition.'

'Ralf, the child is yours — I swear it.'

He turned to her, his dark eyes flashing with merriment.

'Indeed if it were not, after that night in Louis's palace, I would doubt my manhood, my Marian.'

She stooped to kiss him and his hands reached up and tightened on her shoulders. Her tears of relief splashed onto the rich velvet of Gloucester's cloak, and then their lips met in a kiss of greeting.

18

Marian looked up at Ralf apprehensively as they entered the Sanctuary of St. Martin le Grand. Here nobles walked among thieves and murderers, sharing alike the need to remain within this hallowed place which kept them safe from arrest from the King's officers. Ralf smiled at her encouragingly.

'Look not so serious, my love. The Lady Anne will think I beat you. I assure you we are perfectly safe. No man commits further crimes while he lies under the protection of Mother Church.'

'It is so many months since I saw her. They say she has been ill.'

Ralf's brows met in a frown. If it were true that the Lady Anne Neville would make but a frail bride for Duke Richard tomorrow, it was not to be wondered at.

Poor, destitute girl. After Tewkesbury she had been arrested fleeing from the field with Queen Margaret.

Edward had been magnanimous to his fallen enemy. Margaret was conveyed to the Tower to join her ailing husband. Anne had been placed under the protection of her sister, Isobel, Clarence's wife. Isobel too had been weak and it was rumoured that Warwick's elder daughter had not long to live. The protection she had been able to afford her sister was little indeed.

At Compton, where Ralf had taken Marian to await the birth of her child, rumours had reached them, alarming and ugly. Anne had disappeared from the Clarence household. Some feared she had been murdered. Richard of Gloucester had stormed at the King at Westminster. He demanded to wed Anne and that Clarence should reveal to him the truth of her whereabouts. Clarence had cursed him to his face and sworn by the Holy Rood he had no knowledge of Anne or why she had left the house.

Marian had fretted with the desire to go to London but Ralf had hardly recovered and Lady Compton had counselled her to stay quietly at home and await the birth of the heir.

'You can do nothing, Marian. Duke Richard will find her if it is the will of God. Leave matters in his hands and be patient. Your own ordeals have weakened you. For our sakes give yourself rest and peace until you are delivered.'

And so it had been. When her son was born in September she had been thankful she had taken their advice. Richard was a healthy child and Ralf rejoiced that mother and babe had come safely through the travail.

Now, at last, they had comforting tidings from London by a messenger from Gloucester. The Lady Anne had been found in a cook-shop in London. He had conveyed her safely to the Sanctuary of St. Martin and he hoped soon to inform them of his marriage plans.

Tomorrow Anne Neville was to marry Richard of Gloucester in the Chapel of St. Stephen in Westminster. Richard was in haste and they were without the official sanction from Rome, a dispensation given by the Pope to the marriage between cousins. He had determined on no more delays. He had found Anne. She was to be his. The King had decreed it. For these last weeks he had fought doggedly for Anne's right to some share in her father's estates. Clarence had fought equally fiercely to retain them, and indeed he was to keep the greater part, but Anne would have the Yorkshire lands, all she required, and with them her father's favourite castle of Middleham and also Sherriff Hutton.

Ralf touched Marian's hand gently as they reached the door of the small house where Richard had conveyed his intended bride, that she might have peace to make her decision without coercion.

'Go in alone. I will join you after you two have had time to exchange womanly confidences.'

He moved away as the door swung open and Marian was conducted inside. Her heart was touched at sight of the frail, gallant girl who had been her companion for so long. Anne held her hands wide to greet Marian and the two embraced, laughing and crying together in the emotional joy of meeting again after so long a parting.

'Let me look at you, lady.' Marian drew away to look well at her erstwhile mistress. 'You are thinner.'

'And you plumper, my Marian.'

Marian flushed. 'I have not yet regained my figure.'

'And the baby, he is well?'

'He is a wonderful child, very like Ralf.'

'And he is glad and fully recovered?'

'Yes. The wound left him with severe head pains for some time but we are all in excellent health, Lady Compton too. We have left Richard in her capable hands.'

'So you came for my wedding?'

'And I rejoice in it with you, Anne.' Marian remembered another betrothal, so long ago it seemed now, and a shadow crossed Anne's lovely features as if, at this same moment, she too had thought back to the bridegroom who had then stood by her side in the Cathedral at Angers.

'We go to Middleham after the ceremony. Richard has promised.'

Anne seated herself near the fire, pushed aside her embroidery frame, and drew Marian down on a seat by her side.

'Tell me of Compton. You are truly happy, Marian?'

Marian nodded. She was puzzled by Anne's manner. That she was pleased to see her was plain enough but she seemed listless, almost fearful and without joy for her marriage. Marian talked mechanically of Norfolk, of baby

Richard and his birth. Anne's face lit up as she talked of the joy of motherhood, making light of the birth pangs for her friend's dear sake. She told herself that Anne had suffered so terribly that it was understandable that she should fear, though there was no longer need for her to do so.

'Why did you leave Clarence's home, Anne? Did he threaten your safety?'

They had fallen silent for a spell and Marian had decided to be forthright and break this barrier of silence which Anne had appeared to place between them when she attempted to broach what had occurred since their last meeting.

A shudder ran through Anne's slender body. She looked away.

'Yes,' she said at last, 'I heard things, disclosures I would not make even to Isobel. I ran away and found work in the cook-shop. They asked no questions; I needed no experience. They wanted only a scullery maid.'

'And you stayed there — all that time

— at such work?'

Anne's blue eyes clouded with tears. 'I was terrified even then that someone would recognise me.'

'Anne, why did you not appeal to the King? He would have protected you. Or why not to Gloucester?'

Anne looked down at her hands, clasped loosely in her lap. She twisted her fingers nervously.

'I was afraid,' she said simply.

'Of Richard of Gloucester?'

Anne's voice was oddly muffled. 'Richard can be ruthless. He killed Edward of Lancaster on the field. I know he had cause but I cannot forget.'

'The Prince was killed in the pursuit.'

'You have proof of that?' Anne peered at Marian intently.

'No — at least . . . '

'He does not deny it, nor that he is responsible for poor King Harry's death.'

Marian avoided Anne's clear gaze. Too well she realised how this accusation was difficult to defend. The saintly King had died on the night of May

21st so soon after the royal brothers had returned to London from Tewkesbury. The King had died from natural causes, it was said, yet there had been whispers of a wound in his neck. Marian went cold again as she had the first time she had heard of the King's death. Months ago Ralf had whispered of the need for Harry's end — for the peace of the realm, he had said. Gloucester was Constable of the Tower. Had he overseen the King's murder at Edward's command? If so then Edward must be held responsible. She said quietly, 'Richard would do what he believed necessary. You must not expect to marry with a saint. How would Edward of Lancaster and Queen Margaret have dealt with the Yorkist lords?'

There was no answer to this and Anne drew her embroidery frame to her and bent her head over the work.

'Has Gloucester forced you to this match?' Again Marian knew the question to be searching, even impertinent.

There was a pause. Anne lifted her head and her pale face was flushed. 'No, he has left me here under the protection of the Church so that I should be free to choose. Oh I do love him, Marian.' The last words came in a little rush. 'I believe that he will deal well with me, but — but I trust no man. So many have used me, my father, Clarence, Prince Edward and now I do not dare to hope that Richard still cares for me as in the old days at Middleham and Westminster before — before my father . . . ' she paused. 'I would be content if I did not feel that I caused Edward of Lancaster's death. Richard needed him dead — for me. Do you understand? He was so young and at the last he was kind to me. I would not have his blood on my soul.'

At last Marian understood Anne's cry of despair. She longed to go to Middleham and live in peace with her Richard, yet her husband's ghost still walked beside them. There was little she could say to convince her friend. Only

Gloucester himself could win back Anne's trust.

She changed the conversation to matters of dress. What was Anne to wear at the ceremony? So engrossed were they in such talk that the Duke of Gloucester and the King were announced before either realised that visitors had arrived. Marian was relieved to see Ralf in attendance on the King.

Edward was in jovial mood. Anne and Marian curtseyed to the ground. He was delighted with the company. Marian was looking charming in a gown of sapphire velvet and little Anne was certainly greatly improved. He hid his concern that his young brother might not sire a son on such a wife. Her gown of palest green brocade trimmed with cloth of silver enhanced her ethereal beauty. She coughed less, they said, now that she lived in tolerable comfort here in Sanctuary and the fresh cold air of the North would do wonders for her frail constitution. Dickon loved the lass; he deserved his happiness.

'Dickon, I would talk with tomorrow's bride while I have opportunity. Come, Ralf, let us pay our respects to the future Duchess of Gloucester.'

Marian watched as her husband joined His Grace the King in the outrageous flattery that brought yet another flush to Anne's pale cheeks and a smile to her lips. She turned to find Gloucester watching her closely.

'You find her greatly changed?'

'She has suffered much.'

'Aye.' He bit his lips and she noted again the nervous habit of twisting the seal ring on his finger. 'God knows it is my ardent prayer that she should trust me and be happy.'

'She loves you, Duke Richard.'

'But fears me.'

'She has had reason to fear all men.'

'She believes me capable of murder, Lady Marian. Do you?'

Marian looked at him bravely. 'I love you too, My Lord Duke. I do not care.'

His grey eyes expressed amazement

and she reached out and touched the brown velvet of his doublet. 'I believe you will do what is best for those you love and for England. More cannot be demanded of any man.'

'I will not stoop to defend myself or plead.'

'I understand. I wish you all joy, My Lord Duke, as you have given me joy.'

His pale, stern face flushed with pleasure. He gave a grave little bow of acknowledgment and, as the King called them forward at the moment, the time for confidences was ended.

Marian was quiet as she and Ralf returned to their lodging.

Ralf raised one eyebrow in mock consternation. 'Lass, you are in no mood for the wedding rejoicing. What ails you?'

'Nothing, Ralf, I swear it.'

'You'll not have fears for the match? I thought her in love with Gloucester from childhood.'

'She is.'

He grimaced. 'I'll never understand women.'